BEST LOVED BOOKS
FOR YOUNG READERS

Beau Geste

A CONDENSATION OF THE BOOK BY

Percival Christopher Wren

Illustrated by Stan Galli

CHOICE PUBLISHING, INC.

New York

PRODUCED IN ASSOCIATION WITH MEDIA PROJECTS INCORPORATED

Executive Editor, Carter Smith
Managing Editor, Jeanette Mall
Project Editor, Jacqueline Ogburn
Associate Editor, Charles Wills
Art Director, Bernard Schleifer

Library of Congress Catalog Number: 88-63359
ISBN: 0-945260-33-4

This 1989 edition is published and distributed by Choice Publishing, Inc.,
Great Neck, NY 11021, with permission of The Reader's Digest Association, Inc.

Manufactured in the United States of America.

10 9 8 7 6 5 4 3 2

Foreword

IN THE SCORCHED desert wastes a detachment of the French Foreign Legion is approaching the lonely outpost of Zinderneuf. There is a mystery surrounding this doomed fort, and in a very strange way it is linked to the lovely, peaceful English manor of Brandon Abbas. It was here that Beau, Digby, and John Geste grew up, and it was here, one pleasant summer evening of the long vacation, that something happened to change the course of their lives, spinning the thread of fate that bound Brandon Abbas to Zinderneuf.

The man who wrote *Beau Geste* once served with the Foreign Legion himself. Percival Christopher Wren was born in Devonshire, England, a descendant of the Christopher Wren who designed Saint Paul's Cathedral. After attending Oxford he spent five years in travel, working his way as sailor, tramp, schoolmaster, journalist, farm laborer, explorer, hunter, and even as a vegetable vendor in the slums of London.

Eventually chance took him to India, where he remained for ten years; and it was here that he started writing. *Beau Geste* was published in 1924, and it was an instant and runaway success—first as a book, then as a play, and finally as a film.

Although Wren wrote approximately forty books, he is known and loved principally for those, like *Beau Sabreur*, which also deal with the adventures of the Geste family. He died in 1941.

PART I

First told by Major Henri de Beaujolais of the Spahis to George Lawrence, Esq., C.M.G., of the Nigerian Civil Service.

MR. GEORGE LAWRENCE, C.M.G., First Class District Officer of His Majesty's Civil Service, sat at the door of his tent and viewed the African desert scene with the eye of extreme disfavor. There was beauty neither in the landscape nor in the eye of the beholder. The landscape consisted of sand, bur grass and yellow *tafasa* underbrush, and the eye was jaundiced by sun, dust, malaria, and continuous marching in appalling heat.

The fact that only a few more hours of travel through deserts and swamps lay between him and the railhead at Kano, between him and "leave out of Africa," was all that kept George Lawrence on his feet. From that romantic Red City, Kano, the train would take him, after a three days' journey, to the rubbish heap called Lagos, on the West African Coast. There he would embark on the good ship *Appam* and sink into a deck chair with that glorious sigh of relief known in perfection only to those weary ones who turn their backs upon the Outposts and set their faces toward Home.

Meantime, for George Lawrence—worry, frustration, heat, sand flies, mosquitoes, fever, and that great depression which comes of monotony indescribable, weariness unutterable and loneliness unspeakable.

And the greatest of these is loneliness.

BUT, IN DUE COURSE, George Lawrence reached Kano, there to wait for a couple of days for the biweekly train to Lagos. These days he whiled away in strolling about the marketplace, exploring the streets of mud houses, and watching the ebb and flow of varied brown and black humanity at the thirteen great gates in the city's mighty earthen ramparts. Idly he watched the caravans starting out for Lake Chad or Timbuktu and exchanged casual greetings with the camel drivers.

On the platform of Kano Station (imagine a platform at Kano, the ancient, mysterious emporium of Central Africa, with its eleven-mile wall, its hundred thousand natives and twenty white men), George Lawrence was suddenly stirred from his weary apathy by his old friend, Major Henri de Beaujolais of the Spahis.

Lawrence had been at Eton with de Beaujolais and the two occasionally met, as thus, on the Northern Nigerian Railway, or at the house of their mutual friend, Lady Brandon, at Brandon Abbas in Devonshire. Lawrence had great respect for de Beaujolais, and frequently paid him the compliment, "Jolly, you might almost be English"—a bouquet which de Beaujolais received with less concern by reason of his mother's having been a Devonshire Cary.

Now, however, the heavily bearded Spahi officer, arrayed in a high-domed white helmet and what Lawrence considered ill-fitting khaki, looked as truly French as his friend looked truly English. A strong handgrip sufficed for both; but de Beaujolais's charming smile and Lawrence's beaming grin showed their mutual delight.

When the train steamed on from Kano and the two men, stretched opposite each other on the couches of an uncomfortable compartment, had exchanged plans for spending their leave—yachting, golf, the moors, on the one hand; Paris boulevards, Monte Carlo, on the other—Lawrence found that his friend was bubbling over with a long story, which he must tell or die.

"I tell you, my dear George," began the Frenchman, "it is the most extraordinary mystery. I shall think of nothing else until I have solved it, and you must help me. As you are aware, I am literally buried alive in my present job at Tokotu. It is the southernmost outpost of the *Territoire Militaire* of the Sahara, a spot compared with which the loneliest Algerian border hole would seem like paradise. Seconded from my beloved regiment, far from a boulevard, a café, I see the sun rise and set, I see—"

"Get on with the mystery," interrupted Lawrence.

"Well, have you heard of our little post of Zinderneuf, north of your Nigeria? No? Well you hear of it now, for it is where the mystery, indeed the tragedy, took place.

"One hot morning in my quarters at Tokotu, while I was yawning in my pajamas over a *gamelle* of coffee, my orderly comes in babbling of a dying Arab goum (they are always dying, these fellows, if they have hurried a few miles) on a dying camel, who cries at the gate that he is from Zinderneuf, where there is siege and massacre.

"'Then bid the goum not die till I have questioned him,' I call to my orderly, as I leap into my belts and boots. 'And tell the Sergeant Major that an advance party of the Foreign Legion on camels marches in nine minutes. The rest of them on mules.'

"As we rode out of the gate, I gathered from the still dying goum on the still dying camel that a couple of days before a large force of Tuaregs has been sighted at Zinderneuf. The wise *sous-officier*, only recently in charge since the lamented death of his superior, immediately turned the goum loose outside the fort. The goum was to make all speed for help if so much as a shot was fired by either side.

"Standing off on a sand hill, the goum actually saw the force of Tuaregs skirmish up to the oasis and park their camels and surround the fort, pouring in a heavy fire. He estimated them at ten thousand rifles (so I feared that there must be at least five hundred), then wheeled round and rode hell-for-leather for help.

"Anyhow, I was now away with the advance party on swift mehari camels, a mule squadron following and a company of Senegalese on foot led by Lieutenant Saint-Juste. And, in what I flatter myself is record time, we reached Zinderneuf.

"Riding far in advance of my men, I listened for the sound of firing or bugle calls; but I heard nothing. Suddenly, topping a ridge, I came in sight of the fort. It lay below me on the desert plain, near the tiny oasis. There was no fighting, no sign of Tuaregs. The Tricolor flew from the flagstaff, and the fort looked absolutely normal—a block of high mud walls, castellated roof, flanking towers and lofty lookout platform. All was well! The Flag of France had been defended! I waved my kepi above my head and shouted aloud. The fort should know that I, Henri de Beaujolais of the Spahis, had brought relief. I fired my revolver half a dozen times in the air—and then was aware of a remarkable fact. The lookout platform was empty.

"Strange! Incredibly strange, when Tuaregs were known to be about. New as the sous-officier might be to independent command, one would have thought he could as soon have forgotten his boots as his sentry on the lookout platform.

"There must be something wrong. I halted and pulled out my field glasses. Could the Arabs have captured the place, put on French uniforms, left the flag flying, and now be waiting in ambush for a relieving force to ride up to the muzzles of their rifles? Possible—but quite unlike brother Tuareg! No, there were good European faces at the embrasures, not Arab.

"Yet that again was strange. At every embrasure stood a soldier, most of them staring along their leveled rifles—some of them straight at me. Why were they not sleeping the sleep of tired victors? And why did no man move; no man turn to call out that a French officer approached?

"As I lowered my glasses and urged my camel forward, I came to the conclusion that I was expected, and that the officer in charge was showing off a little. He was going to let me find everything as the Arabs had found it—every man at his post and all *klim-bim*. Yes, that must be it. Even as I watched, a couple of shots were fired from the wall. They had seen me! The fellow, in his joy, was almost shooting *at* me, in fact!

"And yet—nobody on the lookout platform. How I would prick that officer's little bubble of swank! And I smiled to myself as I rode under the trees of the oasis to approach the gates of the fort.

"Among the palm trees were little pools of dried blood where men had fallen, showing that the assailants had paid a heavy toll.

I rode out from the oasis and up to the gate. Here half a dozen or so were looking out as they leaned in the embrasures of the parapet. The nearest was a huge fellow with a bushy gray mustache, from beneath which protruded a wooden pipe. His kepi was cocked rakishly over one eye as he stared at me with the other, half closed and leering, and kept his rifle pointed at my head. I was glad he was no Arab, but I thought his joke a poor one and overpersonal.

"'*Congratulations!*' I cried. '*France and I are proud to salute you,*' and I raised my kepi in homage to their victory.

"No one saluted. No one answered. I was annoyed.

"'*Have you no manners?*' I shouted. '*Go, one of you, and call your officer.*' Not a finger nor an eyelid moved. I then addressed myself to old Gray Mustache. '*You,*' I said, pointing up at his face, '*tell your commandant that Major de Beaujolais of the Spahis has arrived with a relieving force. Take that pipe out of your face and step smartly.*'

"And then, my friend, I grew a little uncomfortable. Why did the fellow not move? Why were they all like statues? Why was the fort so silent in the fierce sunlight of the dawn? As in a nightmare, I began to ride round the walls, trying to attract attention.

"I am rather nearsighted, as you know, and it was not until then that I saw that one man, whose kepi had fallen from his head, had a hole in his forehead. He was dead. They were all dead!

"Why were they not sleeping the sleep of tired victors? I had asked myself. They were, all of them! *Mort sur le champ d'honneur!* . . .

"My friend, I rode back to where Gray Mustache kept his last watch and, baring my head, I made my apologies to him, and the tears came into my eyes. Yes, I, Henri de Beaujolais of the Spahis, admit it without shame. I said, '*Forgive me, my friend.*' What would you, an Englishman, have said?"

"What about a spot of tea?" quoth Mr. George Lawrence, reaching beneath the seat for his tiffin basket.

AFTER A DUSTY MEAL, impatiently swallowed by Major de Beaujolais, that gentleman resumed his story.

"Of course, it soon occurred to me that *someone* must be alive. Shots had been fired, and someone had propped up these corpses and arranged them with their rifles in position. Besides, what about the wounded? There is always a bigger percentage of wounded than of killed in any engagement. They must be below in the casern. Well, I would soon solve the problem.

"When my men arrived, I had the alarm and the regimental call sounded by the trumpeter, but still there was no movement. Sending for the *Chef*, as we call the Sergeant Major, I ordered him to make a rope of camel cords, and set a fellow to climb from the back of a camel into an embrasure and give me a hoist up.

"That Sergeant Major is one of the bravest men I know, and his collection of *ferblanterie* includes the *Croix* and the *Medaille* given on the field, for valor. But now he looked queer, and I knew that he was afraid. 'It is a trap, *mon Commandant*,' said he. 'Do not walk into it. Let me go.'

" 'We will neither of us go,' said I, on second thoughts. 'We will send a man in, and if it is a trap, we shall know without losing an officer. Send me that drunk, Rastignac.' And the Sergeant Major rode away.

" 'May I go, mon Commandant?' said the trumpeter, saluting.

" 'Silence,' said I. My nerves were getting on edge. When the Sergeant Major returned with a rope and the rascal Rastignac—whose proper place was in the penal battalions of convicted criminals—I ordered him to climb from his camel onto the roof.

" 'Not I, *mon Officier*,' replied he. 'Let me go to hell dead, not living. You can shoot me.'

" 'That can I,' I agreed, and drew my revolver. 'Ride your camel under that waterspout, stand on its back, climb into the embrasure, then go down and open the gates.'

" 'Not I, mon Officier,' said Rastignac again. I raised my revolver, and the Sergeant Major snatched the man's rifle.

" 'Have you *le cafard?*' I asked, referring to the desert madness. Bred of monotony and hardship, it makes European soldiers do strange things, varying from mutiny and suicide to dancing about naked, or thinking they are lizards or clock pendulums.

" 'I dislike intruding upon a dead company,' replied the fellow.

" 'For the last time—*go*,' said I, aiming between his eyes.

"'Go yourself,' replied Rastignac—and I pulled the trigger. . . . Was I right, my friend?"

"Dunno," replied Lawrence, yawning.

"There was a click, and Rastignac smiled. I had emptied my revolver while approaching the fort, as I have told you.

"'You can live—to be court-martialed,' said I, and I bade the Sergeant Major take his bayonet and put him under arrest.

"'Show this coward the way,' I said to the trumpeter, and in a minute he had sprung to the spout and was scrambling onto the wall. He was *un brave*.

"'Until the gates are opened we will proceed as though the place were held by an enemy,' said I to the Sergeant Major, and we rode back to the oasis. I would have given something to know what each of my men was thinking. Not an eye wandered from the silent fort. Two minutes passed; five, *seven*. What could it mean? *Was* it a trap after all?

"'*That* one won't return!' cried Rastignac with an eerie laugh, and a corporal smote him on the mouth.

"At the end of ten minutes I said to the Sergeant Major, 'I'm going in. Take command. If you do not see me within ten minutes, assault the place.' Then I rode back to the fort.

"I remember thinking as I rode what a fool I should look if, under the eyes of all, I failed to accomplish that difficult scramble, and had to admit my inability to climb up where the trumpeter had gone. However, all went well, and, after an undignified dangling from the spout, I scrambled up and crawled into an embrasure.

"And there I stood, dumbfounded, unable to believe my eyes. The garrison stood with their backs to me, their feet in dried pools of blood—watching, watching. Yet soon I forgot what might be awaiting me below; even forgot my vanished trumpeter and my troop without—*for there was something else*.

"Lying on his back, his sightless eyes outstaring the sun, lay the Commandant, and through his heart was *a bayonet*, one of our thin French bayonets with its single-curved hilt! What do you say to that, my friend?"

"Suicide," replied Lawrence.

"And so did I, until I realized that he had a loaded revolver in one hand, one chamber fired, and a crushed letter in the other! Does a man drive a bayonet through his heart, then pick up a revolver and a sheet of paper? I think not.

"Was it any wonder that my jaw dropped? Evidently he had been a bold, resourceful hero, of a macabre humor. As each man fell, he had propped him up, set the rifle in its place, fired it, and bluffed the Arabs that every loophole was fully manned—guarded by soldiers who could not be killed! No wonder the Arabs never charged. As I realized what he had done and how he had died in the hour of victory, *murdered* by a French bayonet, my throat swelled, and I thought of how France should ring with the news of his heroism, how every Frenchman should clamor for the blood of his murderer. Only a sous-officier of the Legion, but a hero for France to honor. . . . And I would avenge him! Such were my thoughts, my friend, as I realized the truth—what are yours?"

"Time for a spot of dinner," said George Lawrence, starting up.

NEXT MORNING, AS THE TWO lay awake on their bedding, de Beaujolais lit a cigarette and fixed his friend with an earnest gaze.

"Well, George, *who killed him*—and why? As I stood on that roof, I vowed to get to the bottom of the mystery. Promptly drawing my revolver, I loaded it and walked to the door. As I was about to descend I looked at each of the watchers in turn. I was glad to see that each man had his bayonet, for I had not really supposed that one of them had stabbed his officer, then gone back to his post and died on his feet! Next, I raised my weapon and descended the stairs—expecting I know not what in that sinister stillness that had swallowed up my trumpeter. And what do you think I found, my friend?"

"Dunno," said George Lawrence.

"*Nothing*. No one and nothing. Not even the man who had fired the two shots of welcome! The place was shut tight. The casern was as orderly as when the man left it—the *paquetages* on the shelves, the bedding folded and straight. There had evidently been

8

room inspection just before the attack. The stores were untouched—rice, biscuits, coffee, wine—nothing was missing. . . ."

"Except a rifle," grunted Lawrence.

"My friend, you've said it! Where was the rifle belonging to the bayonet that had murdered the officer? I remembered that the bayonet had been driven through the sous-officier's breast in a slightly *upward* direction from front to back. As it could not have been thrown thus from outside the fort, I was driven to conclude that the officer must have been bayoneted by someone in the fort, by one of his own men. The revolver in his hand with an empty cartridge case in one of its chambers confirmed this conclusion. I asked myself, Does a man conducting the defense of a blockhouse waste time taking potshots with a *revolver* when he has a score of rifles on hand? Of course not. That revolver was fired at one of his own soldiers, the one who murdered him and who then, finding himself to be the sole survivor, detached the rifle from the bayonet and fled from the fort.

"But why did this murdering soldier not *shoot* his officer, and then calmly await the arrival of the relieving force? If he were lusting for vengeance because of some real or fancied wrong, surely he would have shot his superior through the head, propped him up with the rest, and accepted congratulations for having conceived the whole scheme of outwitting the Arabs. Wouldn't he, George?"

"I would," replied George, scratching his head.

"Now there was only one other soldier who was not propped up at his post. He lay on his back with closed eyes and folded hands. Whoever had been doing the ghastly work of corpse drilling had overlooked him—or was about to set the dead man up when the final tragedy occurred. It may have been that the brave sous-officier was going to arrange this very corpse when he was attacked. Or, it may have been that the man who had fired the two shots was about to do this—but if so, what had become of him?

"My head spun. I felt I was going mad. Then I said to myself, *Courage, mon brave!* Go calmly up to that roof again, and just take another look. I turned to ascend the stair, then suddenly I remembered something else. Where was my trumpeter? '*Trompette!*' I shouted. I rushed to the door leading to the courtyard. '*Trompette!*' But there was not a sound.

"Then, in something like panic, I ran to the gates, lifted the bars and dragged them open—just as my good Sergeant Major was giving the signal to join the assault! The sound of his voice, after a quarter of an hour in that House of Death, made me realize that I urgently yearned for some . . ."

"Breakfast," said George Lawrence.

BATHED AND FED, WE SMOKED a cheroot in silence. Then de Beaujolais spoke. "George, *mon vieux*, do you believe in spirits?"

"I believe in whisky," George Lawrence replied.

"Because the only solution my Sergeant Major could offer was just that. 'Spirits!' he whispered, when I told him that the sous-officier had been murdered, apparently by a corpse, and the trumpeter had vanished into thin air.

"'Sergeant Major Dufour,' said I, 'post vedettes round the place, and let the men fall out and water their beasts at the oasis. Fires may be lighted and *soupe* made, but in an hour's time all are to be on grave-digging fatigue. If a vedette gives the alarm, all are to enter the fort immediately—otherwise no one is to set foot inside, except you and me. When you have given your orders, we will look into this affair together.'

"While he was gone on this business I went back to the roof. I preferred the sunlight while I was alone. Perhaps I was not quite myself. I had ridden all night; I was perilously near cafard myself; and this experience had shaken me a little. I gazed at the face of the dead sous-officier. Not too pleasant a sight—contorted with rage and hate . . . And it was getting hot. There were flies. . . .

"Then I looked again at the other man who was lying near. Undoubtedly someone had reverently laid him out. His eyes had been closed, his head propped up on a pouch, his hands folded upon his chest. Why had he received such different treatment? Then I glanced at his kepi, lying near him. Its lining, newly ripped, was protruding, and the band was turned down and outward. It was as though something had been torn out of the lining.

"And from that cap I looked instinctively at the paper crushed in the left hand of the dead officer. I know not why I connected these two things, but I was about to take the paper from the rigid fist when I thought, No! Everything shall be done in order. I will touch nothing until the Sergeant Major arrives and I have a witness.

"But without touching the paper, I could see that the writing was in English! A paper in English, in the hand of a dead French officer in the heart of the Territoire Militaire of the Sahara!"

"Perhaps the bloke was English," suggested Lawrence, yawning. "I have heard that there are some in the Legion."

"No. A typical Frenchman of the Midi—a stoutish, florid, blue-jowled fellow. Thousands like him in Marseille."

"And the recumbent chap?" said Lawrence.

"Ah—quite another affair! He might well have been English. Just the type turned out by your public schools and universities. Here was a little glimmer of light, a possible clue. Had this Englishman killed the sous-officier while the latter tore some document from his cap? Obviously not. The poor fellow's bayonet was in its sheath. And, if he *had* done it, how had he got himself shot and then had himself arranged with his hands across his chest?

"No, there must be a soldier of the garrison missing—he must have taken his rifle and left his bayonet in the sous-officier, instead of shooting him and awaiting praise.

"Then I heard the Sergeant Major ascending the stairs.

"'All in order, mon Commandant,' reported he with a salute, then fell to eyeing the corpses. 'Even to half-smoked cigarettes in their mouths!' he whispered. *The fallen who were not allowed to fall.* But where in the name of God is Jean the Trumpeter?'

"'Tell me that, Chef, and I will fill your kepi with twenty-franc pieces,' said I.

"The Sergeant Major blasphemed, crossed himself, then said, 'Let us get out of here while we can.'

"'Are you a sergeant major or a young lady?' I inquired—and rated him soundly for feeling exactly as I did myself; and the more I said, the more angry and unreasonable I grew.

" 'Did your Excellency make a search?' he asked, rebukingly polite, as at last I got a hold of myself.

" 'What need to search for a living man, in a small place into which he has been sent to open a gate? *Mon Dieu*, he has legs, he has a tongue in his head! If he were here, wouldn't he *be* here?'

" 'Murdered perhaps.'

" 'By whom? Beetles? Lizards?'

"He shrugged his shoulders, and pointed to the sous-officier. That one had not been murdered by beetles or lizards!

" 'Yes,' said I, 'but now we'll reconstruct this crime, first reading what is on this paper,' and I opened the officer's stiffened fingers, releasing the letter along with a crumpled envelope.

"Now George, mon vieux, prepare yourself. You are going to show a little emotion, my frozen Englishman!"

Lawrence smiled faintly.

"It was a most extraordinary document. On the envelope was *To the Chief of Police of Scotland Yard and all whom it may concern.* And on the paper, *Confession. Urgent. Please publish.* Under that I read, *I hereby confess that it was I, and I alone, who stole Lady Brandon's great sapphire known as Blue Water. . . .*"

"What!" shouted George Lawrence, jumping to his feet.

"Aha, my little George!" The Frenchman smiled, gloating. "We do not yawn now, do we?"

George Lawrence stared at his friend, incredulous. *"But that is Lady Brandon's jewel!* Are you being funny, de Beaujolais?"

"I am telling you what was written on this paper."

"Good God, man! *Lady Brandon!* . . ." muttered Lawrence. "Do you mean to say that the Blue Water has been pinched—and that the thief was in the Foreign Legion?"

"I don't mean to say anything—except to tell my tale, the dull little tale that has bored you so, my George," replied de Beaujolais, with a malicious grin. "But perhaps you begin to realize how shocked I was when I read that paper with Lady Brandon's name on it, there in the middle of the Sahara and sticky with blood."

"Go on, old chap," begged Lawrence, sitting down again. "I apologize for my recent manners. Please tell me everything, then let us thrash it out. . . . Lady Brandon! . . . The Blue Water stolen! . . ."

"No need for apologies, my dear George," said his friend, smiling. "If you seemed a little bored at times, it only gave me the greater zest for the denouement, when you should hear your . . . our . . . friend's name come into the story. But there is another surprise to come."

"For God's sake, get on with it," replied Lawrence, now all animation and interest. "More about Lady Brandon, is it?"

"Indirectly, *mon cher* George. For that paper was signed—*by whom?*" asked the Frenchman, leaning forward, tapping his friend's knee and staring at that bewildered gentleman with narrowed eyes. Then into the ensuing silence he slowly and deliberately dropped the words, *"By Michael Geste!"*

"By *Michael Geste!*" said the astounded Lawrence. "Her nephew? You don't mean to tell me that 'Beau' Geste stole her sapphire and slunk off to the Legion?"

"I don't mean to tell you anything, my friend, except that the paper was signed 'Michael Geste.'"

"Was the recumbent Englishman he?"

"I do not know, George. I saw two or three boys and two very beautiful girls once at Brandon Abbas years ago. This man might have been one of them. The age would be about right. Then, again, this man *may* have had nothing to do with the paper. Nor any other man on that roof, except the sous-officier—and he was certainly not Michael Geste. He was a man of forty or more."

"Michael would be about twenty," said Lawrence. "He was the oldest of her nephews. . . . But, my dear Jolly, the Gestes don't *steal!* . . . Oh, I am going to put some ice on my head."

"I have wanted a lot of ice on my head the last few weeks, George. What, too, of the murdered sous-officier and the vanished trumpeter?"

"Oh, damn your trumpeter and sous-officier," was the explosive reply. "Michael Geste! . . . Lady Brandon . . . Forgive me, old chap, and continue the story . . ." and George Lawrence lay back and stared at the roof of the carriage, thinking of Lady Brandon, who, to him, was the only woman in the world.

AND, AS THE TRAIN RUMBLED ON through the sweltering coastlands toward Lagos, Major de Beaujolais did continue.

"Well, my George, figure me there, with this new astoundment to accompany the mystery of an inexplicable murder and an inexplicable disappearance.

"And then, 'What is in the paper, mon Commandant?' asked the Sergeant Major.

"'The confession of a thief. He stole a famous jewel,' I replied. 'Now come with me and we will make one more search below, then déjeuner and a quiet, sensible discussion of the facts before we bury these fellows. Then I'm going to detail an *escouade* of men as garrison and return to Tokotu. I shall leave you in command here until we get orders and reliefs.'

"The Sergeant Major looked dubious. '*Here*—for weeks!' he said softly.

"We made our tour below, and, as before, nothing unusual met the eye. There was no sign of the trumpeter, alive or dead. I was past wonder. I accepted things. This was a place where commandants are murdered by nonexistent people, soldiers vanish like smoke, and English letters concerning one's friends are found in the hands of dead Frenchmen. Very good. We would 'carry on,' as you say, and do our duty. We passed out of the gate, and I proceeded to the oasis for déjeuner.

"You do not want to hear all the futile theories I constructed—those explanations that explained nothing. But it may interest you to hear that I was faced that evening, on top of my other pleasures, with a military mutiny."

"Good Lord!" ejaculated Lawrence.

"Yes. At four o'clock I ordered the Sergeant Major to fall the men in. I would read off the new garrison for Zinderneuf. But, strangely, instead of stepping smartly off about his duty, the Sergeant Major hung fire.

"'Well?' said I sharply.

"'There is going to be trouble, mon Commandant. Sergeant Lebaudy says that Corporal Brille says that the men say . . .'

"'Name of the Name of the Name of Ten Thousand Thundering

Tin Devils!' I shouted. 'You say that he says that they say that she says. *Va t'en, grand babillard!* I'll be on parade outside those gates in ten seconds, and if you and your gibbering chatterboxes aren't there at attention . . .' and my poor Sergeant Major fled.

"I was the more angry at his news, for I had subconsciously expected something of the sort. I had no doubt that Rastignac had begun it—he who had faced instant death rather than enter the place. There is nothing so infectious as *that* sort of panic.

"Well, it was one more fact to accept, but if the will of these ignorant, superstitious clods conflicted with the will of Henri de Beaujolais, there were exciting times ahead. I would teach my little dogs to show their teeth—and I rode over to the fort. There I bade Dufour and Lebaudy select an escouade of the worst men in the company. They should garrison either Zinderneuf, or else the grave that had been dug for those 'fallen who were not allowed to fall.' Sergeant Major Dufour called the men to attention, and they stood like graven images, the selected escouade on the right, while I made an eloquent funeral oration for that brave band to whom we were about to give a military funeral.

"Then, when the selected garrison got the order to march into the fort and bring the dead out for burial—they did something quite otherwise. As one man they laid their rifles on the ground and stood at attention! The right-hand man, a grizzled veteran, took a pace forward, saluted, and with wooden face said, 'We prefer to die with Rastignac.'

"Here was rank mutiny. I had hardly expected quite this. As I was deciding what to do, with every eye upon me and a terrible tension drawing every face, the Sergeant Major approached and saluted. I eyed him coldly. With his back to the men, he whispered, 'They won't enter the fort, mon Commandant. For God's sake do not give the order. They will shoot you and desert en masse. . . . A night's rest will work wonders. Besides, Lieutenant Saint-Juste and the Senegalese will be here by midnight.'

"'And would you like to ask these fellows to spare us till the Senegalese come?' I whispered back. Then, looking from him to the men, I said loudly, 'You are too merciful, Sergeant Major.

However, in consideration of the excellent march the men have made, I will do as you beg and give these cafard-stricken fools till moonrise. At moonrise our motto is, *Work or die!* Till then, all may rest. After then, the dead will be buried and the fort garrisoned.'

"I rode back to the oasis, hearing as I did so the voice of the Sergeant Major exhorting the men and concluding with the order, '*Rompez!*' He joined me a few minutes later.

"'They'll never do it, mon Commandant,' said he. 'They'll fear the place worse than ever by moonlight. In the morning we could call for volunteers to accompany us. Then the Senegalese . . .'

"Patting him on the shoulder, I bade him send me four or five of the most influential men in the company—leaders of different cliques, if there were any. I would point out to them the results of disobedience and mutiny. I would speak of heroism and discipline. I would then send them back among their fellows—and abide the issue. . . .

"Well, I talked to the men whom Dufour brought in that manner, and then, just as they turned to go, I had another idea. Suppose some of them would volunteer to go over the fort with me, see for themselves that there was nothing to be afraid of, then report to their fellows that all was well. Their statements, and the airs of superiority which they would inevitably give themselves, might counteract Rastignac's influence and their own superstitious fears.

"'Wait a moment,' said I. 'Is there a man of courage among you—a man like the trumpeter, brave enough to enter an empty fort with me?'

"They looked sheepish for a moment. Someone murmured, 'And where *is* Jean the Trumpeter?' Then I heard a curious whispered remark: 'Gee! I sure would like to see a ghost, Buddy,' and the reply: 'Yeah, Hank, and I'd like to see our pals again.'

"Two men stepped forward and saluted. One was a giant and the other not more than five feet in height. Both had clean-shaven leathery countenances—biggish noses, mouths like a straight gash, and big chins. By their speech they were Americans.

"'Isn't there a *Frenchman* among you?' I asked the rest.

"Another man, a big sturdy Gascon he looked, saluted and joined the Americans. Then what they call mob psychology came into play, and the others did the same.

"Good! I would take them round the fort, as though doing honor to the dead, and then I suddenly remembered . . ."

"The murdered sous-officier," said George Lawrence.

"Exactly, George! These fellows must not see him lying there with a French bayonet through him! I must go in first alone, re-move the bayonet, and cover his face. Then it would be assumed that he had been shot. Yes, that was it. . . .

"I bade the Sergeant Major march them over to the fort, then mounted a mule and rode quickly across to the gate. Dismounting, I hurried up the dark staircase to the roof, and there as I emerged into the light I stood and rubbed my eyes. For a moment I felt faint and just a little in sympathy with those poor superstitious fools of the escouade. For, my dear George, the body of the sous-officier *was no longer there!* Nor was that of the recumbent Englishman!"

"Good God!" ejaculated Lawrence.

"Yes, that is what I said. What else was there to say? *Were* there really evil spirits in this cursed desert? Had I dreamed that a sous-officier had lain here, with a French bayonet through him?

"Then I think my temperature went up a few degrees from the mere hundred and two one disregards, for I remember thinking that perhaps a living man was shamming dead among these corpses. I remember going round from corpse to corpse and questioning them. One or two I took by the arm, shouted at them, and shook them until they fell to the ground, their rifles clattering.

"Suddenly I heard the feet of men upon the stair, and pulled my-self together. The Sergeant Major and the Legionnaires came out on the roof. I managed to make a suitable little speech as they stared round in amazement, the most amazed of all being the Sergeant Major, who gazed at the smeared pool of blood where the sous-officier had lain. The two Americans seemed particularly interested, and appeared to be looking for comrades among the dead. But quickly I bade Dufour take them all back to the oasis. As he dis-appeared, last, down the stair, I called him back and we were alone together. Simultaneously we said the same words: '*Did you move it?*'

I laughed loudly, if not merrily, and the Sergeant Major produced an oath remarkable even for the Legion.

"'Quite so, Chef,' said I. 'Life grows a little complicated.'

"'I'll give a complicated death to this farceur, when I find him,' growled he as he clattered down the stair. Soon after, I heard his voice below, as he led the group of men across the courtyard. Then I made my own way back to the oasis. In fact, I fled. . . .

"Well, George, mon vieux, what do you think happened? Did the escouade obey and enter the fort like lambs, or did they refuse and successfully defy me?"

"Give it up, Jolly," was the reply. "I can only feel sure that one of the two happened."

"And that is where you are wrong," said de Beaujolais. "They neither obeyed and entered, nor disobeyed and stayed out!"

"Good Lord!" ejaculated Lawrence. "What then?"

And this time it was the Frenchman who suggested a little refreshment.

"WELL, IT WAS THE LAST EVENT on that remarkable program, mon cher," resumed de Beaujolais a little later. "A very appropriate and suitable one too. . . . 'An open-air entertainment concluded with fireworks,' as the reporters of fêtes champêtres say."

"Fireworks? Rifle fireworks do you mean?" asked Lawrence.

"No, just fireworks. Works of fire . . . I will tell you. . . .

"I let the moon get well up, then sent for the Sergeant Major, and bade that good fellow to parade the men as before, with the fort a hundred paces in their rear, the garrison escouade on the right of the line. This party would either march into the fort, or else the remainder would be ordered to right form and shoot them where they stood. If the remainder did not obey, I would at once give the order to pile arms. If they did this, as they might, from force of habit, they would immediately be marched off to the oasis by the noncommissioned officers and marched back to Tokotu under escort of the Senegalese, to await court-martial. If they did not pile arms, the noncommissioned officers were to come at once to me, and we would prepare to sell our lives dearly.

"It was a weird and not unimpressive scene. That sinister fort, silver and black; the frozen waves of the ocean of sand; the men, like statues, inscrutable and still.

"What would they do? Would my next words be my last? As I faced the men, I was acutely interested, yet felt like a spectator, impersonal and unafraid. I was about to witness a thrilling drama, depicting the fate of one Henri de Beaujolais, quite probably his death. I hoped he would play a worthy part on this moonlit stage. I was calm. I was detached. . . ."

George Lawrence sighed and struck a match.

"I cast one more look at the glorious moon and took a deep breath. If this was my last order, it should be given in a deep voice, clear and firm. Above all firm. And as my mouth opened, and my lower jaw moved in the act of speech—I believe it dropped, George, and my mouth remained open.

"For, from the fort, there shot a tongue of flame!

"'*Mon Dieu! Regardez!*' cried the Sergeant Major, pointing. Every head turned, and in the silence I heard him whisper, '*Spirits!*'

"That brought me to myself sharply. 'Yes, imbecile!' I said. 'They carry matches and indulge in arson! Where is Rastignac?' For it was obvious that someone in the fort had set fire to something highly inflammable. As I watched, another column of fire burst in a different place.

"'I told Corporal Brille to tie him to a tree,' said Dufour.

"I did not think it could be Rastignac's work, for he would not have entered the place even had he been at liberty to do so. Nevertheless, I ordered: 'See if he is still there—and make sure that everyone else is accounted for.'

"It was useless to detail a squad to put the fire out. In the desert, when a place burns, it burns. And, mon Dieu, how it burned! Anyway, to tell the truth, I did not care how completely it *did* go! This fire would be the funeral pyre of those brave men, it would keep my fools from mutiny, and it would purge the place of mystery. Incidentally, it would also save my life and military reputation.

"I gave the order to face about and stand at ease. The men should watch it burn. Perhaps they would then realize that human agency is required for setting a building on fire—and, moreover, whoever was in there had to come out or be cremated. They should see him come. But who? *Who* and *why?*

"All stood absolutely silent, spellbound, until suddenly a rifle cracked, again and again. From the sound, the firing was toward us. The Arabs were upon us!

"Far to the right and to the left more shots were fired. Bullets whistled overhead and I saw flashes from a distant sand hill. No one was hit—the fort being between us and the enemy—but in less time than it takes to tell I had the men turned about and making for the oasis. There we should have cover and water, and if we could hold the devils until they were between us and Saint-Juste's Senegalese, we would avenge the garrison of that blazing fort.

"They are grand soldiers, those Legionnaires, George. They are to infantry what my Spahis are to cavalry. It warmed one's heart to see them double back to the oasis, steady as on parade, every man select his cover and go to ground, his rifle loaded and leveled. Our camel vedettes rode in soon after. Two of them had had a desperate fight, and two of them had seen rifle flashes and fired at them before returning to the oasis. They had thought the Arabs were burning the fort. In a few minutes the whole place was silent and apparently deserted. Nothing but a burning fort, and a black brooding oasis where nothing moved.

"What were the Arabs doing now? Probably preparing to rush us at dawn from behind the nearest sand hills. They would lull us into a sense of security, then come down upon us as we slept. But what if our waiting rifles caught them at fifty yards, and the survivors turned to flee—on to the muzzles of the Senegalese?

"I bethought me of getting into communication with Saint-Juste. I reckoned he would soon be drawing near, and it was quite possible that he might run into the Arabs anyway. If he came in darkness, after the flames at the fort had died down, he might march straight into a trap.

"It would be a good messenger that could reach Saint-Juste. There was the track to find and follow, and there were the Arabs to face. On the whole it might be better to send two.

"I went round the oasis until I found the Sergeant Major, and asked for a couple of men of the right stamp for my job. I was not surprised when he suggested the two Americans who had been in the fort with me. He recommended them as men who could use the stars, and were good resourceful scouts.

"When I asked the big slow giant and the little quick man if they would like to undertake this duty, they seemed more than ready. I found them of quick intelligence, and both repeated lucidly what I wanted them to say to Saint-Juste: that he might be able to attack the attackers at dawn, just when they were attacking me.

"The two left on camels from the side opposite the fort, and after they had disappeared over a sand hill, you may imagine with what anxiety I listened for firing. But all was silent.

"After two or three hours of this unbroken stillness, the fire having died down in the fort, I felt certain there would be no attack until dawn. All who were not on guard duty slept, and as I strolled silently round the oasis, waiting for sunrise, I thought over the incredible events of the day. My mind grew clearer as my body grew weaker, and I decided that all this was the work of a madman concealed in the fort, and now burned to death.

"But, George, although my lunacy theory might account for these hopelessly lunatic proceedings—it hardly accounts for the sous-officier having a confession that Michael Geste had stolen a jewel, does it?"

"It does *not*, my son, and that, to me, is the most remarkable fact in your most remarkable story," replied Lawrence.

"Well, I decided to leave it at that," continued de Beaujolais, "and soon afterward the sky grew gray in the east. Before dawn we silently stood to arms, and when the sun peeped over the horizon we beheld Saint-Juste's Senegalese skirmishing beautifully toward us! There wasn't so much as the smell of an Arab for miles.

"Saint-Juste had not seen a living thing—not even the two scouts I had sent out to meet him. Nor did anyone else ever see those two brave fellows again. I have often wondered what their fate was—Arabs or thirst.

"Anyway, I soon learned that one of Saint-Juste's scouts had heard rifle shots in the direction of Zinderneuf, and Saint-Juste had increased his pace until he knew he must be near his goal. Then, fearful of an ambush, he had decided to halt for the rest of the night and feel his way forward in attack formation at dawn.

"He had done well, and while the weary troops rested I told him all that had happened. He is a man with a brain, this Saint-Juste, ambitious and a real soldier, a little dark pocket Hercules of energy and force. When I had finished my account, and, having fed, we were sitting against a fallen palm trunk with coffee and cigarettes at hand, he said, 'Suppose your trumpeter killed the sous-officier?'

"'Mon Dieu!' said I. 'That never occurred to me. But why should he, and why use his bayonet and leave it in the body?'"

"'Well—as to why he *should*,' replied Saint-Juste, 'it might have been revenge. Some injustice, when he was under this man at Sidi-bel-Abbès or elsewhere.'

"'No,' I said. 'Impossible. Why had not the sous-officier rushed up to the lookout platform when I approached? I fired my revolver to let them know that relief had come, and two answering rifle shots were fired! Why did he not rush down to the gates and throw them open?'

"'Wounded and lying down,' suggested Saint-Juste.

"'He was not wounded,' said I. 'That bayonet, and nothing else, had done his business.'

"'Asleep,' suggested the Lieutenant, 'absolutely worn out—and thus his enemy, the trumpeter, found him, and drove the bayonet through his heart. He would have blown his brains out, but the shot would have been heard. Therefore he used the bayonet, and he fled when he realized that the bayonet would betray him.'

"'And the officer's revolver, with *one* chamber fired?' I asked.

"'Oh—fired during the battle.'

"'And the paper in his left hand?'

"'I do not know.'

"'And who fired the two welcoming shots?'

"'I do not know.'

"'And how did the trumpeter vanish across the desert before the eyes of my company?'

"'I do not know.'

"'Nor do I,' I said.

"And then Saint-Juste sat up suddenly. 'Mon Commandant,' said he, 'the trumpeter did *not* escape! He murdered the sous-officier, then hid himself. It was he who removed the two bodies when he was again alone in the fort. He may have had some idea of turning the stab into a bullet wound and returning to the company with some tale of cock and bull. But, since you had already seen the bayonet, he determined to set fire to the fort, burn all evidence, and rejoin in the confusion caused by the fire. He could swear that he had been knocked on the head and only recovered in time to escape the flames kindled by whoever had clubbed him. This is no more improbable than the actual facts of the case.'

"'Quite so. But why did he not rejoin in the confusion?'

"'Well, suppose the sous-officier did shoot at him with the revolver and wounded him so severely that by the time he had completed his arson he was too weak to walk. He fainted from loss of blood and perished in the flames that he himself had kindled. A splendid example of poetic justice.'

"'Magnificent,' I agreed. 'The only flaw is that *we should have heard the shot*. In that heavy silence a revolver would have sounded like a seventy-five.'

"'True,' agreed Saint-Juste, a little crestfallen. 'The man was mad then. He did everything, then committed suicide or was burned alive.'

"'Ah, my friend,' said I, 'you have come to the madman theory, eh? So had I. But now I will tell you something. The trumpeter did *not* do all this. He did *not* murder the sous-officier, for that unfortunate had been dead *for hours*, and the trumpeter had not been in the place ten *minutes!*'

"'That's that,' said Saint-Juste. 'Let's try again.' And he tried again—very ingeniously too—but he could put forward no acceptable theory.

"We were both, of course, weary to death and more in need of twenty-four hours' sleep than twenty-four conundrums. But I do not know that I have done much better since.

23

"As I rode back to Tokotu with my bout of fever, at every stride of my camel my head opened and closed with a shattering bang to the tune of, *Who killed the Commandant, and why, why, why?* till I found I was saying it aloud. I am saying it still."

CHAPTER 2: GEORGE LAWRENCE GOES TO BRANDON ABBAS

Passengers on the ship *Appam*, from Lagos to Birkenhead, were interested in two friends who sat side by side in Madeira chairs, or walked the deck in constant company. It appeared the two had something on their minds, for, save for brief intervals of eating, sleeping and playing bridge, they discussed interminably. When the Englishman contributed to the discussion, he spoke most often of a bareheaded man and a paper, speculating as to the identity of the former and the authorship of the latter. The Frenchman, on the other hand, talked more of a murder, a disappearance and a fire.

"How long is it since you heard from Lady Brandon, Jolly?" inquired George Lawrence, one glorious and invigorating morning, as the *Appam* plowed the blue Bay of Biscay.

"Oh, years," was the reply. "I was at Brandon Abbas for a week about six or seven years ago. I haven't written a line since the letter of thanks after the visit. Do you correspond with her regularly?"

"Er—no. I shouldn't call it regularly," answered George Lawrence. Then, with a simulated yawn, "Are you going to Brandon Abbas this leave?"

"Well—I feel I ought to go and take that incredible document, but it doesn't fit in with my plans at all. I could post it to her, of course, but it would mean a devil of a long letter of explanation, and I loathe letter writing."

"I'll take it if you like," said Lawrence. "I shall be near Brandon Abbas next week. And knowing Michael Geste, I confess I am curious."

Major de Beaujolais knew that "curious" was not exactly the right word. His friend had been stirred to the depths of his soul, and had given an exhibition of emotion such as he had never displayed before in all de Beaujolais's experience of him. He smiled to himself as he gravely replied: "But excellent, mon vieux! That would be splendid. You could say that, while the document is probably a canard, I nevertheless think that she ought to have it."

"Just that," agreed Lawrence. "Of course 'Beau' Geste never stole the sapphire, or anything else; but a document like that ought to go to her and Geste, as their names are mentioned."

"Certainly, *mon ami*. And if the stone *has* been stolen, the paper might be a clue to its recovery. Handwriting, for example, is a splendid clue. She could please herself as to whether she should put it in the hands of your Scotland Yard."

"Righto, Jolly," was the reply. "I'll drop in there one day. Though it looks to me as though the thief, the jewel and the story all ended together in the burning of Zinderneuf fort."

"Mon Dieu! I never thought of it before. The biggest and finest sapphire in the world may be lying at this moment among the burned-out ruins of Zinderneuf fort!"

"So it may," agreed Lawrence, and for a moment he had visions of devoting this leave to jewel hunting, and returning to Brandon Abbas with three quarters of a million francs' worth of crystallized alumina in his pocket. He daydreamed awhile—of himself, Lady Brandon, and the sacrifice of his leave to the making of a great restoration, one which would elevate him in her eyes and make him worthy of her admiration. Sacrifice his leave? Nay, if necessary, his career, his whole life.

Lawrence was awakened from his reverie by the voice of de Beaujolais. "Queer that it never got into the papers, George. I should have thought every paper would have had an account of the theft of a famous jewel like that."

"Yes, it is strange, but I should certainly have seen it if it had. Probably the damned thing was never stolen at all."

And, his friend agreeing, they dropped the subject of Beau Geste, the Blue Water, and the secret of Zinderneuf.

On parting in London, Major de Beaujolais handed a document to George Lawrence, who promised to deliver it, and also to keep his friend informed as to any developments of the story.

THE FOLLOWING DAY, AS HIS HIRED CAR sped along the country road that led to Brandon Abbas, George Lawrence's heart beat like that of a boy going to his first love tryst.

Had she married him a quarter of a century ago, when she was plain Patricia Rivers, he would still have loved her, though he would not still have been in love with her. As it was, he had never been anything but in love with her from the time when he had taken her refusal like the man he was, and sought an anodyne by working in Central Africa.

As the car entered the gates, he actually trembled, and his bronzed face was changed in tint. He fingered his tie and tugged at his mustache. Driving round a shrubbery-enclosed square at the back of the house, he stopped at a big porch with a hospitably open door. From there, he looked into a well-remembered paneled hall— he almost nodded at the two suits of armor that stood on each side of its big, doorless doorway—and then he looked toward the wide spiral staircase at the far end. Suddenly, he pictured her descending it from three stories above with slow and stately grace, just as she had done on that first occasion when he had come to visit her again after her marriage. She had been married seven years and he had been seven years in exile. He had entered this hall, half in the hope that seeing her the wife of another man would cure him of the foolish love that kept him a lonely bachelor, but he could still remember that sudden moment of perverse gladness as she had come down the stairs and he had realized that he loved her even more than before.

Again and again, at intervals, he had visited the shrine, and nothing seemed to have changed. Yes—there was the fifteenth-century chest on which she had once sat beside him while they waited for the dogcart to take him to the station and back to Africa, and her hand had rested so kindly in his, as he had tried to find something to say—something other than what he might not say. . . .

Quickly, he pulled the chain of the doorbell, and the butler appeared. "Hallo, Burdon!" said Lawrence.

"Why, Mr. George, sir!" replied the old man, coming forward and looking unwontedly human. "This is a real pleasure, sir." (It was—a real five-pound note too, when Mr. Lawrence departed.)

"Her Ladyship is at the Bower, sir, if you'd like to come straight out." He knew that the visitor was always welcome.

"How is Lady Brandon?" inquired Lawrence as he followed Burdon through the house.

"She enjoys very good health, sir—considering."

"Considering what?"

"Everything, sir," was the noncommittal reply.

The visitor smiled to himself. A good servant, this. Then, "Is Mr. Michael here?" he asked.

"No, sir, nor none of the other young gentlemen," was the reply. (Was there anything unusual in the old man's tone?)

Crossing a rose garden, the pair followed a path that came out onto a square of velvet turf. On two sides rose the great old trees of a thickly forested hill; and, from the front, the hillside fell away to a famous view.

By a wicker table a lady reclined in a chaise longue. She was reading a book and her back was toward Lawrence, whose heart missed a beat, then made up for it by redoubling its speed.

The butler coughed at the right distance, and, as Lady Brandon turned, announced the visitor, placed a wicker chair, and faded from the scene.

"*George!*" said Lady Brandon in her soft deep contralto, with a pleased brightening of her gray eyes and a flash of beautiful teeth. She extended both hands and he kissed them in a curiously reverent manner.

"My dear Patricia," he said, looking long at the unlined yet mature and determined face before him—that of a woman forty-five years old, of strong character and aristocratic breeding. "Yes, you are positively as beautiful as ever."

"And you as foolish, George. Sit down. Tell me why you have again disobeyed me and come here before your wedding. Or—or—are you married, George?" she asked, smiling.

"No, Patricia, I am not married," said Lawrence, relinquishing her hands slowly. "I have disobeyed you because I hoped you might be in need of my help. I mean, I feared you might be in need of help, and hoped that I might be able to give it."

27

Lady Brandon fixed a penetrating gaze on Lawrence—a possibly wary one, he felt. "In need of help, George? How?"

"Well—it is a longish story, but I need not inflict it on you if you'll tell me if Beau Geste is all right, and—er—the Blue Water—er—safe and sound and—er—all that, you know."

"What?" There was no doubt now as to the alarm on Lady Brandon's face. "What *are* you talking about, George?"

"Beau Geste, and the Blue Water," replied Lawrence. "If I appear to be talking through my hat, there is method in my madness, dear."

"There's madness in your method," replied Lady Brandon a trifle tartly, and added: "Have you seen Michael, or what?"

"No, I have not seen him, Patricia. But I have a document that purports to be his confession that he stole the Blue Water."

"Then it *was* . . ." whispered Lady Brandon, greatly perturbed. "But how and where did you get this confession? Tell me quickly."

"It's a long story. It was found by Henri de Beaujolais at a place called Zinderneuf in the French Sudan, in the hand of a dead man—"

"Not *Michael!*" interrupted Lady Brandon.

"No—a Frenchman. An *adjudant* in charge of a fort that had been attacked by Arabs. But look here, *has* the sapphire been stolen, Patricia, and—er—excuse the silly question—*is* this Beau's writing?" He produced the dirty piece of paper from his pocket.

Lady Brandon looked at it, her face hard, a puzzled frown marring the smoothness of her forehead. She read it, then looked out across the green, as though communing with herself and deciding how to answer. "Tell me the whole story from beginning to end, George," she said at last, "if it takes you the weekend. But tell me this quickly. *Do* you know anything more than you have told me about Michael or the Blue Water?"

"I know nothing whatever, my dear," was the reply, and the speaker thought he saw a look of relief on his hearer's face. Obviously there was something wrong, and in connection with Beau Geste, too. He wished she would be less guarded. It would be so easy to say: My dear George, the Blue Water is in the safe in the

Priest's Hole as usual, and Michael is in excellent health; or, on the other hand: The Blue Water has vanished and so has Michael.

But her pleasure was her pleasure, and if she chose to be secretive even with *him*, who had unswervingly loved her from his boyhood, so be it. His was only to serve in any way she deigned to indicate. . . .

As they strolled back to the house, Lady Brandon slipped her hand through Lawrence's arm, and it was quickly imprisoned. He glowed with the thought that he might hear her say, when all his tale was told: Help me, George. You are a tower of strength and I am in great trouble.

"You aren't looking too well, George, my dear," she said, as they entered the wood.

"Lot of fever lately," he replied.

"Give it up and come home, George." He turned quickly toward her, and she added, "And let me find you a wife."

Lawrence sighed and ignored the suggestion. "Where is the good Sir Hector Brandon?" he asked, with casual politeness.

"Oh, in Kashmir, I believe, thank you, George. Have you brought a suitcase?"

"I—er—am staying at the Brandon Arms, and have one there," admitted Lawrence.

"And how long have you been at the Brandon Arms?"

"Five minutes."

"You must be tired of it then, dear," commented Lady Brandon. "I'll send Robert for your things."

THAT EVENING, AFTER A poignantly delightful dinner à deux, George Lawrence told Lady Brandon all that Major de Beaujolais had told him, adding his own suggestions and theories. As she listened, her eyes scarcely left his face. But she offered no opinion and asked only a few questions.

Even when the time came for him to leave on the following day, she had not once admitted, or even implied, that the Blue Water had been stolen. His own scrupulous care to avoid questioning her made this easy for her. But was it really possible, he wondered, that Lady Brandon's own nephew, Michael Geste, had actually stolen the stone and that, regarding it as a family disgrace, she was trying to shield him? It would be so like her.

"Come and rest on this chest a moment, Patricia," he said, as he waited in the hall for the arrival of his car, "to give me my orders. You will make me happier than I have been since you told me that you liked me too much to love me."

Lady Brandon seated herself beside him. "We have sat here before, George," she said, smiling, and, as he took her hand: "My dear, this is what I want you to do for me. *Nothing* at all. The Blue Water is not at Zinderneuf, or anywhere else in Africa. Where Michael is I do not know. What that paper means, I cannot tell. Thank you so much for wanting to help me, and for asking no questions—but now, good-by, my dear friend. . . ."

"Good-by, my dearest dear," said George Lawrence, sorely puzzled, and went out to the door a sadder but not a wiser man.

As the car drove away, Lady Brandon stood in deep thought, pinching her lip. "To think of that now!" she said. "'Be sure your sins . . .' The world *is* a very small place. . . ."

PART II

CHAPTER I: BEAU GESTE AND HIS BAND

"I THINK THAT IF Very Small Geste were allowed to live, he might retrieve his character and find a hero's grave," said the Lieutenant.

"And what would he do if he found a hero's grave?" inquired the Captain.

"Pinch the flowers and sell them, I suppose. As for retrieving his character, it is better left where it is—if it is not near water used for drinking purposes—"

"Oh, *please* let him live," interrupted Faithful Hound. "He is very useful, if only to try things on."

I was grateful to Faithful Hound for daring to intercede for me, but felt she was rating my usefulness somewhat low.

"Well, we'll try bread and water on him, then," said the Captain after a pause. "We'll also try a flogging," he added, on seeing my face brighten, "and the name of Feeble Geste. Remove it."

I was removed by the Lieutenant, Ghastly Gustus and Queen Claudia, that the law might take its course. It took it, while Faithful Hound wept and Queen Claudia watched with interest.

I used to dislike the bread and water even more than the "six of the best," which was the flogging administered, more in sorrow than in anger, by the Captain himself. The opprobrious name only lasted a day, but it was perhaps the worst punishment of all. It kept one in the state of unblessedness, disgraced and outcast.

This was part of the Law as laid down by the Captain, and beneath his Law we lived, desiring his praise and rewards more than we feared his blame and punishments.

The Captain was my brother, Michael Geste, later and generally known as "Beau" Geste, by reason of his beauty, brilliance and general distinction. He was a person of irresistible charm, and his charm was enhanced by the fact that he was as enigmatic as he was forceful. He was incurably romantic, but of bulldog tenacity. If he suddenly did some ridiculously romantic thing, he did it thoroughly and completely, and he stuck to it until it was done. Aunt Patricia, whose favorite he was, said that he combined the reckless courage of a youthful d'Artagnan with the staunch tenacity of a wise old Scotchman. Little wonder that he exercised an extraordinary fascination over those who lived with him.

The Lieutenant, my brother Digby, was his twin, a quarter of an hour his junior, and his worshiping shadow. Digby had all Michael's qualities, but to a less marked degree. He was "easier," both upon himself and other people. He loved fun and laughter, but, above all, loved doing what Michael did.

I was a year younger than the twins. At school we were known as Geste, Small Geste, and Very Small Geste, and I was, indeed, Very Small in all things compared with my brothers, to please whom was my chief aim in life. Probably I transferred to them the affection that would have been given my parents; but we were orphans, and lived our lives between school and Brandon Abbas.

Our aunt, Lady Brandon, did more than her duty by us, but certainly concealed her love, except toward Michael. Childless herself, all her maternal love was given to him and Claudia, an extraordinarily beautiful girl whose origin was, so far as we were concerned, mysterious, but who was vaguely referred to as a cousin. She and Isobel Rivers, a niece of Aunt Patricia, spent a good deal of their childhood at Brandon Abbas, Isobel being, I think, imported as a companion for Claudia when we were at school. She proved an excellent companion for us also, and soon earned the honorable title of Faithful Hound.

Augustus Brandon, nephew of Sir Hector, often came during holidays, in spite of the discouragement of the name Ghastly Gustus and our undisguised disapproval. One could not love Augustus. He was too like Uncle Hector. Also, he was too disposed to presume upon his being the heir. However, Michael dealt with him faithfully, neither sparing the rod nor spoiling the child.

I do not remember the precise crime that had led to my trial, but I recollect the incident for two reasons. One is that on this same day I achieved the permanent title of Stout Fella, when, inverting the usual order, Pride came after the Fall. The other was that on that evening we had the privilege of seeing the Blue Water, the great sapphire which Uncle Hector had given Aunt Patricia as a wedding gift. I believe his great-grandfather had "acquired" it when soldiering in India.

This sapphire was the loveliest, most fascinating thing I have ever seen. I could look at it for hours; it always gave me a curious longing to put it in my mouth, or hold it to my nose like a flower; for so beautiful an object seemed to demand the exercise of all five senses. When I first heard the charitable remark, "Sir Hector Brandon bought Patricia Rivers with the Blue Water and now owns the pair," I felt that both statements were true. After all, possession of the Blue Water must have been Aunt Patricia's only reason for marrying a man like Uncle Hector. Yet the fact remained that the stone was still owned by Uncle Hector; Aunt Patricia having married him was forbidden even to wear it; she could only look at it occasionally, like anybody else.

My degree of S.F. (Stout Fella) I earned in this wise. One of Michael's favorite pastimes was "Naval Engagements." Two stately ships, with sails set and rudders fixed, were simultaneously shoved forth from the edge of the lily pond by the Captain and the Lieutenant. They were crowded with lead soldiers, and each bore a battery of three brass cannon. To each loaded cannon was attached a fuse, and, at the Captain's word, the fuses were lighted as the ships were launched from their harbors. The Captain presided over the ship that flew the Union Jack, and the Lieutenant over the one that carried the Tricolor of France.

There was a glorious uncertainty of result. Each ship might receive a broadside from the other, one alone might suffer, or both might blaze ineffectually into the blue. After the broadsides had been exchanged, we all sat and gloated as the ships glided on, wreathed in battle smoke, perhaps with riddled sails and splintered hulls. I was then privileged to wade out, like Gulliver at Lilliput, and bring the ships to harbor, where their guns were reloaded and the voyage repeated.

On this great day, the first combat was ideal. The ships converged, the guns fired, splinters flew, soldiers fell, and the ships remained locked in a death grapple.

"Fetch 'em in, Feeble Geste," said Michael, and, tucking up my trousers, I waded in and sent the ships back to port.

The next round was more one-sided, for only one of the French ship's guns fired. The big gun amidships and the stern-chaser swivel gun were improperly fused.

I waded in again, turned the French ship and, with a mighty bang, her big gun went off, and I took the charge in my leg. Luckily it was a single buckshot, but as I emerged from the pond blood oozed from a neat blue hole, and Faithful Hound uttered a doglike howl of horror. Claudia asked to be informed exactly how it felt.

"Just like being shot," I replied. "I am going to be sick."

"Do it in the pond then," requested the Captain, producing his pocketknife and a box of matches. "Now," he continued, holding the blade in the flame, "will you be gagged or chew on a bullet? I don't want my surgery disturbed by your beastly yells."

"I shall not yell, Captain," I replied with dignity.

"Sit on his head, Dig," said Michael to the Lieutenant; but waving Digby away, I turned on my side and offered up my limb.

"Hold his hoof then," ordered the Captain.

It was painful beyond words; but I bit my knuckles and refrained from kicking by realizing it was impossible with Digby sitting on my leg and Claudia standing on my foot.

After what seemed a long time, I heard Michael say, "Here it comes." Then, a cheer from the Band announced the recovery of the buckshot. "Shove it back in the gun, Dig," said the Captain. "Isobel, sneak up to the bathroom and bring me the scratch muck."

The Faithful Hound, mopping her tear-bedewed face, sped away and soon returned with the scratch muck (the bottle of antiseptic lotion, packet of boric lint and roll of bandage). Michael made a really excellent job of dressing the wound. He then raised me to seventh heaven by solemnly conferring upon me, in perpetuity, the title of Stout Fella, in that I had shed no tears and uttered no sounds. Further, he awarded me the signal honor of a full-dress Viking's Funeral.

A Viking's Funeral cannot be solemnized every day, for it involves, among other things, the destruction of a longship. The dead Viking is laid upon a pyre in the center of his ship, his spear and shield beside him; his dog is slaughtered and its body placed in attendance. Then the pyre is lighted and the ship sent out with all sails set. On this occasion, the offending French ship was dedicated to these obsequies. A specially selected lead soldier, after being endowed with the name of *The Viking Earl, John Geste*, was laid upon a matchbox full of explosives, with a small (china) dog at his feet. Then the ship was drenched with paraffin. We bared our heads, Michael solemnly uttered the beautiful words, "*Ashes to ashes and dust to dust; if God won't have you the devil must*," and, applying a match, shoved the ship out into the middle of the pond.

The leaping flames consumed the mast and sail, and we stood silent, envisaging the horrors of a burning ship at sea.

As the vessel burned down to the water's edge, then disappeared with a hiss, Michael broke silence with words that Digby and I were to remember many years later.

"*That's* what I call a funeral!" he said. "Compare that with being stuck ten feet down in a beastly cemetery. Cripes! I'd give something to have one like that when my turn comes."

"Righto, Beau," said Digby. "I'll give you one, old chap."

"So will I you, Dig, if you die first," replied Michael to his twin, and they solemnly shook hands upon it.

THAT EVENING WE WERE variously employed in the schoolroom when Burdon, the butler, came and told us that we could go into the drawing room.

Claudia and Isobel were there, the former talking in a very grownup way to a jolly-looking foreign person, to whom we were presented. We were thrilled to discover that he was a French cavalry officer on leave from Morocco, where he had been fighting.

"We must get him up to our camp tomorrow," whispered Michael, as we gathered round a glass dome under which, on a white velvet cushion, lay the Blue Water sapphire. We looked at it in silence, and I distinctly had the feeling it would not be good to stare too long at that wonderful concentration of color. It seemed alive, a little sinister.

"May we handle it, Aunt Patricia?" asked Claudia, and, as usual, she got her way.

Aunt Patricia lifted off the glass and handed the jewel to the Frenchman, who gave it to Claudia. "That has caused we know not what of strife and bloodshed," he said. "What a tale it could tell!"

"Can you tell tales of strife and bloodshed, please?" asked Michael, and soon we were all begging him to tell us about his fighting. He ranked second only to the Blue Water as a center of attraction.

The following afternoon, after lunch, Claudia exercised her fascinations upon the stranger, and brought him to our camp in the Bower, a clearing in the woods near the house. Here he sat on a log and thrilled us with tales of the Spahis, the French Foreign

Legion, the *Chasseurs d' Afrique*, and other romantically named regiments. He told us of desert warfare, of Arab cruelties, of hand-to-hand combats, veiled Tuaregs, mirages, sandstorms, and the wonders of Africa. He showed us fencing tricks and feats of swordsmanship, until, when he left us, after shaking our hands and kissing Claudia, we were his, body and soul.

"I'm going to join the French Foreign Legion when I leave Eton," announced Michael suddenly. "Get a commission, then join his regiment."

"So am I," said Digby, of course, and I agreed.

Next day we went back to school at Slough.

As our school days went by, my heart ached more and more for Aunt Patricia. Poor woman, she had contracted an alliance with Sir Hector Brandon as one might contract a disease. The one alleviation was the affliction's intermittence; for this monument of selfishness was generally anywhere but home, he being a mighty hunter and usually in pursuit of prey, biped or quadruped, in distant places. It is a good thing to have an aim in life, and Sir Hector's was to kill one of every species of beast in the world, and court a woman of every nationality.

As children, we did not realize, of course, what Aunt Patricia suffered at the hands of this man, but as we grew older it was impossible to avoid knowing that he was universally hated, and that he bled the estate shamelessly in order to enjoy himself abroad. Children might die of diphtheria because of faulty drains, or old people of chills because of leaking roofs, but Sir Hector's yacht and Sir Hector's lady friends would lack for nothing. And Lady Brandon had to remain at home to face the music—whether growls of wrath or cries of pain.

But we boys and girls were exceedingly fortunate: a happy band who followed our leader Michael, carefree and joyous.

The feat of Michael's that impressed us most was his sustaining the role of a Man in Armor for what seemed an appallingly long time. (It was nearly long enough to cause my death!)

One wet afternoon, he had the brilliant idea of dressing up in one of the suits of armor in the outer hall. Nothing loath, we, his henchmen, with much ingenuity and more string, cased the knight in his armor. He was just striking an attitude and bidding a caitiff to die when the sound of a motor horn anachronistically intruded and the Band dispersed like rabbits. Michael stepped up on the pedestal and stood at ease, Digby fled up the stairs, the girls dashed into the drawing room, Augustus rushed down the corridor, and I dived into an old chest in the hall.

There I lay as though screwed down in a coffin; pride forbade me to crawl forth. I was suffering horribly—and the next thing I knew, I was lying on my bed and Michael was smiting my face with a wet sponge while Digby dealt kindly blows upon my chest and stomach.

When sufficiently recovered, and rebuked for being such an ass, I was informed that Aunt Patricia had driven up with a "black man"—mystery of mysteries!—and had confabulated with him right in front of the Man in Armor, afterward speeding the "black man" away again in her car. We were much intrigued, for Michael would not say a word beyond that such a person had come and gone again, and that he himself had remained so still that not a creak or clank had betrayed him.

In the universal admiration for this feat, my own poor perform- ance in preferring death to discovery passed unpraised until Digby, who was an expert bugler, took down his old coach horn from the wall and blew what he said was an "honorific fanfare of heralds' trumpets" in recognition of our joint tenacity.

In spite of Michael's reticence, we others discussed the visit of the "black man" in all its bearings. Arriving at no conclusion, however, we were driven to the theory that the strange visitor was in some way connected with a young maharajah—who had been at Eton. We remembered him as having been a splendid athlete, very devoted to Michael but, at the same time, as a rather strange sort of fellow. Aunt Patricia had once welcomed him to Brandon Abbas at Michael's request, and when he saw the Blue Water *he actually and literally fainted*.

I suppose the sight of the sapphire was the occasion rather than the cause, but it was uncanny beyond words, the more so since he never uttered a sound, and neither then nor afterward said one syllable on the subject of the great jewel.

And so we lived our happy lives at Brandon Abbas, when not at prep school, at Eton, or later, at Oxford.

CHAPTER 2: THE DISAPPEARANCE OF THE "BLUE WATER"

THEN, ONE FINE AUTUMN EVENING, life suddenly and unexpectedly changed. The act of one person altered the lives of all of us, and brought suffering, exile and death in its train.

On this evening, so ordinary yet so fateful, we sat after dinner in the drawing room of Brandon Abbas. Present were Aunt Patricia, Claudia, Isobel, Michael, Digby, Augustus Brandon and myself.

Aunt Patricia asked Claudia to sing, but she excused herself on the score of being out of sorts and not feeling like it. She certainly looked pale and somewhat below her usual sparkling standard. For some days she had seemed preoccupied and worried, and I wondered if her bridge debts and dressmakers' bills were the cause.

With her wonted desire to be helpful, Isobel went to the piano, and for some time we listened while my aunt knitted, Claudia frowned, Augustus tapped his cigarette case with a cigarette he dared not light, Digby turned the leaves of a magazine, and Michael watched Claudia.

Presently Isobel rose from the piano, and Claudia said, "Oh, Aunt, *do* let's have the Blue Water down for a little while. I haven't seen it for ages."

"Rather!" agreed Michael, and Aunt Patricia said she would get it. Only she and Uncle Hector knew the secret of opening the Priest's Hole, and I believe it would have taken an extraordinary burglar to have discovered it. (Michael, Digby and I had spent countless hours, with the consent of our aunt, trying to find the trick, but without success.)

Aunt Patricia disappeared for a time, and then returned, carrying the sapphire on its cushion under the dome. She placed it on a table beneath the chandelier with its countless cut-glass pendants and circle of electric bulbs, and there it lay, its glowing blue fascinating us as we gazed upon it.

"What *is* the Blue Water worth, Aunt Patricia?" asked Claudia.

"To whom, dear?" was the reply. "If somebody were anxious to buy it, I suppose he'd try to find out the lowest sum that would be considered."

"Supposing you were going to sell it, what would you ask?"

"I certainly am not going to sell it," said Aunt Patricia, in a voice that should have closed the conversation. She had that day received a letter from her husband announcing his early return from India, and it had not cheered her at all.

"I heard someone say that Uncle Hector was offered thirty thousand pounds for it," said Augustus.

"Did you?" replied Aunt Patricia.

"Oh, let me kiss it," cried Claudia.

Aunt Patricia, raising the dome, picked up the sapphire and examined it as though she had never handled it before. She looked through it at the light. She then passed it to Claudia, who fondled it awhile. We all took it in turn, Augustus throwing it up and catching it as he murmured, "Thirty thousand pounds for a bit of glass!" When Michael got it, I thought he was never going to pass it on. He weighed and rubbed and examined it more in the manner of a dealer than an admirer of the beautiful. Finally, Aunt Patricia put it back on its cushion and replaced the cover.

Michael began to talk about Indian rajahs and their marvelous historical jewels, and I was just bending over the table, peering into the depths of the sapphire, when suddenly, as occasionally happened, the lights failed and we were plunged in darkness.

"What's Fergusson up to now?" said Digby, alluding to the chauffeur, who was responsible for the generator.

"It'll come on again in a minute," said Aunt Patricia. "Don't wander about, anybody, and knock things over."

Somebody brushed lightly against me as I stood by the table.

"Ghosts and goblins!" said Isobel in a sepulchral voice. "Who's got a match? A skeleton hand is about to clutch my throat! I can see—"

"Everybody," I remarked, as the light came on again. We blinked at each other in the dazzling glare.

"Saved!" said Isobel, with an exaggerated sigh of relief. Then, as I looked at her, she stared openmouthed, pointing.

The white velvet cushion beneath the glass cover was bare. The Blue Water had vanished.

Aunt Patricia broke the silence. "*Your* joke, Augustus?" she inquired, in a tone that would have made an elephant feel small.

"*Me?* No, Aunt! I swear! *I* never touched it."

"Well—there's someone with a sense of humor all his own," she observed, and I was glad that I was not the misguided humorist. Also I was glad she had regarded the joke more probably Augustan than otherwise. "You were standing by the table, John," she continued. "Are you the jester?"

"No, Aunt," I replied with feeble wit, "only the Geste."

Digby and Michael both pleaded innocent, and so did the girls.

Lady Brandon eyed the six of us severely. "Let us agree that the brilliant joke has been carried far enough, shall we?" she said.

"Put the brilliant joke back, John," said Augustus. "You were the only one near it when the light went out."

"Suppose *you* put it back, Ghastly," said Digby, and his voice had an edge on it.

"I haven't *got* the beastly thing," shouted Augustus ferociously. "It's one of you three rotters."

The situation was rapidly becoming unpleasant. My aunt's lips were growing thinner, and her eyebrows beginning to contract toward her high-bridged nose.

"Look here, sillies!" said Isobel. "I'm going to turn the lights out again for two minutes. Whoever played the trick is to put the Blue Water back—then no one will know who did it," and she walked to the door and flicked the light switch. "Everybody keep still except the villain," she said.

It occurred to me that it would be interesting to know who had played this joke and told a lie. I therefore stepped toward the table and laid my hand on top of the glass dome. Whoever came to return the sapphire must touch me, and him I would seize.

Perfect silence reigned in the big room.

"I can't do it, my boots creak," said Digby suddenly.

"I can't find the cover," said Michael.

"Another minute, villain," said Isobel. "Hurry up."

Then I was conscious of someone's breathing, and I felt a faint touch on my elbow. A hand came down against my wrist—and I grabbed. My left hand was round a coat sleeve, and my right grasped a wrist. I was glad it was a man's arm. Ghastly Gustus, of course . . . It was just the sort of thing he would do. But I was surprised that he did not struggle. He kept perfectly still.

"I am going to count ten, and then up goes the light," came the voice of Isobel from the door.

"It's all right, I've put it back," said Digby.

"So have I," said Michael, close to me.

"And I," echoed Claudia.

Isobel switched on the light, and I found that my hands were clenched on the right arm of—Michael!

I was more surprised than I can say. It was as unlike him to do it as it was to flatly deny having done it. And my surprise increased when Michael, looking at me queerly, remarked:

"So it was *me*, John, was it? Oh, *Feeble* Geste!"

I felt absurdly hurt, and turning to Augustus said, "I apologize, Gussie. I admit I thought it was you."

"Oh, don't add insult to injury," he replied. "Just put the beastly thing back, and stop being funny."

I turned and looked at the cushion. It was still empty! "Oh, shove it back, Beau," I said.

Michael gave me one of his penetrating looks.

"Put it back, Beau, and let's have a dance," said Isobel. "May we, Aunt?"

"Certainly," said Aunt Patricia, "as soon as the humorist in our midst has received our felicitations."

We all stood silent.

"Now stop this fooling," said Lady Brandon. "Unless the Blue Water is produced at once, I shall be very seriously annoyed," and her foot began to tap.

I SHALL NOT FORGET THE SUCCEEDING HOURS in a hurry—six people suspecting one of the other six, and the seventh person pretending to do so.

My aunt quickly brought things to a clear issue. She walked to a chesterfield that stood in a big window recess and there seated herself with the air of a queen on a throne.

Nobody spoke.

"Since the fool won't leave his folly . . ." began my aunt. "Come here, Claudia. Did you take the Blue Water?" She laid her hand on Claudia's arm, drew her close, and looked into her eyes.

"No, Aunt," she said. Then again, "No, Aunt."

"Of course not," said Aunt Patricia. "Go to bed, dear." And Claudia departed, not without an indignant glance at me.

"Come here, Isobel," continued my aunt. "Have you touched the Blue Water since I put it back in its place?"

"No, Aunt, I have not."

"I am sure you have not. Go to bed. Good night."

Isobel turned, then stopped. "But I might have, Aunt, if the idea had occurred to me. It's just a joke, of course."

"Bed!"

Isobel departed with a kind glance at me.

Aunt Patricia turned to Augustus. "Come here," she said, staring into his shifty eyes. "If you have got the Blue Water and give it to me now, I shall not say another word about the matter. Have you?"

"I swear to God, Aunt—"

"You need not swear to God, nor to me, Augustus. Yes or no."

"*No*, Aunt! I take my solemn oath I—"

"John," said my aunt, "do you know where the stone is?"

"No, Aunt," I replied, and added, "nor have I touched it since you did."

She favored me with a long look, which I was able to meet calmly, I hope not rudely. As I looked away, my eyes met Michael's. He was watching me queerly.

Then came Digby's turn. He said quite simply that he knew nothing about the jewel's disappearance, so that left Michael. He was the culprit, or else one of us had told a lie.

"Michael," said Aunt Patricia very gravely and sadly, "I'm sorry. More so than I can tell you. Please put the Blue Water back, and I will say no more. But I doubt whether I shall feel like calling you Beau for some time."

"I *can't* put it back, Aunt, for I haven't got it," said Michael quietly, and my heart bounded.

"Do you know where it is?"

"I do not, Aunt."

"Have you touched the sapphire since I did?"

"I have not, Aunt."

"Do you know anything about its disappearance?"

"I only know that *I* have had nothing to do with its disappearance," answered my brother.

My aunt stared at Michael, then said, "This is inexpressibly disgusting. One of you is a despicable liar and, apparently, a common thief. I am still unable to think the latter so I shall leave the cover where it is and lock all the doors of this room at midnight. I shall keep the keys, except the key of that door there. That one I shall put in the brass box above the fireplace in the outer hall. The servants will have gone to bed and know nothing of its whereabouts. I ask the liar to return the sapphire during the night, relocking the door, and replacing the key in the brass box. If this is *not* done by the time I come down tomorrow, I shall have to conclude that the liar is also a thief, and act accordingly. For form's sake I shall tell Claudia and Isobel." Then she rose and swept from the room without a good-night to any of us.

I think we each heaved a sigh of relief as the door shut behind her. But now what?

Digby turned upon Augustus. "Oh, you unutterable cheese mite," he said, apparently more in sorrow than in anger. "I think debagging is indicated."

Augustus glared from one to the other of us like a trapped rat. "You lying swine!" he shouted. "Who was by the table when the light came on again? Who was grabbing who?"

I looked at Michael, and Michael at me.

Augustus had never defied either of my brothers before. I expected to see him suffer promptly, but Michael did the unexpected, as usual.

"Why, I believe the little man's innocent after all," he said.

"You *know* I am, you damned hypocrite!" shouted Augustus.

Digby's hand closed on the scruff of the boy's neck. "If I've accused you wrongly, Gussie, I'll make it up to you. But if we find you *did* do it—oh, my little Gussie . . . !"

"And if you find it was Michael, John or yourself?" sneered the disheveled and shaking Augustus.

Michael looked hard at me and I at him.

"Look here," said Digby, "presumably the thing is in the room. Aunt wouldn't pinch her own jewel, and no one supposes one of the girls did it. That leaves us four. Find it, Gussie, and I'll swear that *I* put it there."

Digby began throwing cushions from sofas, moving footstools, and generally hunting about, while he encouraged himself, and presumably Augustus, with cries of "Good dog! Sic 'em, pup!" and joyful barks.

We searched minutely, but it was clear that the Blue Water was not in the room, unless far more skillfully concealed than would have been possible in those few minutes of darkness.

"Well, that's that," said Digby at last.

"Better tidy up a bit before we go," suggested Michael. "Servants'll smell a rat if it's like this tomorrow."

We three straightened the room, while Augustus sullenly watched us.

"Come to the smoking room, you two?" said Digby to Michael and me, when we had finished.

"Yes—go fix it up, cads," urged Augustus. "For two damns I'd sit in the hall all night, and see who comes for that key."

"Either that lad's innocent or he's a really accomplished young actor," I observed, looking after the retreating Augustus, as we crossed the hall and made our way to the smoking room.

Once there, we threw ourselves into deep leather armchairs and produced pipes. "Well, my sons, what about it?" said Michael, poking up the fire.

"Pretty go if the thing isn't there in the morning," said Digby. "I wonder if she'd send to Scotland Yard?"

"Fancy a fat mystery merchant prowling about here and questioning everybody!" said Michael.

"A bit rough on Aunt too—apart from the thirty thousand pounds," said I.

"Reconstruct the dreadful crime," suggested Digby. "Wash out Aunt and the girls."

"And Gussie," said Michael. "Nothing but injured innocence would have given him the pluck to call us hypocrites."

"You're right, Beau," agreed Digby. "'Sides, young Gus hasn't the guts to pinch anything valuable."

"Well—that leaves us three," said I.

"You can count me out, old son," grinned Digby. "Search me."

"Then that leaves you and me, John," said Michael.

"Yes, it leaves me and you." Again we stared at each other. "I did not take the Blue Water, Beau."

"*Nor did I*, John."

"Then there's a misdeal somewhere," remarked Digby, rising. "Anyhow—it'll be put back tonight, and I've had enough today." He chuckled. "I say, what a lark to pinch the key and hide it."

"Don't be a fool," said Michael. "Let's go to bed," and we went with our usual curt good-nights.

But it was easier for me to go to bed than to go to sleep. I tossed and turned. Eliminating the others, there remained only Michael and me. How *could* it be Michael? Had *I* done it myself? Such was my mental condition by this time that I actually entertained the idea. In fact, I got up and searched my clothes—but of course I found nothing. Hour after hour of reiterated argument brought me nearer to the conclusion that either Augustus or Michael was the culprit. Having arrived at this point, I delivered myself of the unhelpful verdict, *I believe Augustus isn't, and Michael couldn't be!*

I went back to bed and made another resolute effort to go to sleep—a foolish thing to do, as it is one of the best ways of ensuring wakefulness. Eventually, at four o'clock in the morning, I decided to reassure myself that the Blue Water had been put back. I got out of bed, put on my robe and slippers, lit a candle, and made my way down the stairs, through the central hall and into the outer hall. Avoiding the protruding sword hilt of a figure in armor, I went up to the big stone fireplace. On the mantel was the ancient brass box in which my aunt had placed the key. Only she hadn't— or someone had removed it—for the box was empty!

Was this a trick of my aunt's to catch the guilty one? If so, presumably I was caught. I was reminded of the occasion many years before, when she had entered the schoolroom and said, "The naughty child that has been in the stillroom has got jam on its chin," and my foolish hand promptly went to my face to see if, by some mischance, it were jammy.

Well—the best thing to do now was to fade ere the trap closed. I turned, wondering whether Aunt Patricia were watching, and reentered the center hall. At that moment I saw someone coming toward me. He or she carried no light, and could identify me, the candle being in front of my face.

"Well, Gussie," said I. "Cold morning."

"Well, John. Looking for the key?" said Michael's voice.

"It's not there, Beau," I answered.

"No, John," said he quietly. "It's here," and he held it out toward me.

"Beau!"

"John!" he mocked me.

A wave of disgust passed over me. What *had* come over my splendid brother? "Good night," I said, turning away.

"Or morning." And, with a short laugh, he went into the outer hall. I heard him strike a match, then followed the rattle of the key and the clang of a falling lid. He had evidently thrown the key into the box and dropped the lid without any attempt to avoid noise.

I went back to bed and, the affair being over and the mystery solved, fell into a broken sleep.

I WAS AWAKENED at the usual time by David, the under footman, with my hot water. "Half past seven, sir," said he; "a fine morning when the mist clears."

"Thank you, David," I replied, and sat up.

What was wrong? Of course—that affair last night, and Michael's fall from his pedestal. Well, there are spots on the sun, and no man is always himself. I dressed and went downstairs.

In the dining room the fire was blazing merrily and a delicious smell came from the sideboard, where covered silver dishes sat on platforms over spirit lamps. The huge room—with its long windows, its warm-tinted Turkey carpet, its paneled walls and arched ceiling—was a picture of solid, settled comfort.

Digby was wandering about with a plate of porridge in one hand, a busy spoon in the other. Augustus was at the sideboard removing cover after cover, adding sausages to eggs and bacon.

"Good effort, Gus," said Digby, eyeing the piled mass. "Shove some kedgeree on top."

"Had it," said Augustus. "This goes on top of the kedgeree."

Isobel was sitting in her place, and I went to see what I could get for her. As I stood by her chair, she put her hand up to mine and gave it a squeeze.

"I'll wait for Aunt Patricia, John," she said.

At that moment, the door opened and Claudia entered, followed by Michael. She looked very white and Michael very wooden and reserved. Michael foraged at the sideboard for Claudia and then went to the coffee table. He took the coffeepot and the milk jug from their tray and held them poised one in each hand over the cup. His face was inscrutable and his hands absolutely steady—but something was wrong. He looked up and saw me watching him.

"Morning, bunface," quoth he. "Sleep well?"

"Except for one unpleasant dream, Beau."

"H'm." He returned to his place beside Claudia, and as he seated himself Aunt Patricia entered the room.

We rose—then stood petrified. One look at her face was sufficient. As she stopped halfway from the door, I knew what she was going to say.

"I request that none of you—*none* of you—leave the house today," she said. "Unless, that is, one of you cares to say, even now, 'A fool and a liar I am, but a criminal I am not!'"

No one moved. "Very well," continued Lady Brandon. "I will have no mercy. The thief shall pay a thief's penalty—*whoever* it may be." She fixed us with her cold, angry gaze. "One other thing: the servants know nothing of this, and they are to know nothing. We will keep it to ourselves—as long as possible—that one of you is a treacherous, lying thief."

Michael spoke. "Say one of us four, please, Aunt Patricia."

"Thank you, Michael," she replied cuttingly. "I will apply to you when I need your help in choosing my words."

"I think you might say *one of you three brothers*," Augustus remarked.

"Hold your miserable tongue," said Lady Brandon. Then, "As I was saying, the servants are to know nothing—until, of course, the police have the story, and the newspapers are adorned with the portrait of one of your faces." Once again her scornful glance swept us in turn. "Has none of you anything more to say?" None of us did. "Very well! No one leaves this house." And with that she went out, closing the door behind her.

"You foul, filthy, utter cads!" sputtered Augustus.

"Cuts no ice, Gus," said Michael, in a perfectly friendly voice. "Run along and play." Then turning to the girls, he said, "Do me a favor, Queen Claudia and Faithful Hound. Go with him, and put this wretched business out of your minds. You have my absolute assurance that it will be settled today."

"How?" said Claudia.

"Never mind how. Just believe and rest assured. Before you go to bed tonight, everything will be as clear as crystal."

"Or as blue as sapphire," said Digby. "By Jove! I've got an idea—a theory! . . . My dog Joss was alarmed at the sudden darkness, jumped on a chair, wagged his tail, knocked over the cover, reversed his engine, smelled round to see what he'd done, found nothing, yawned in boredom—and inhaled the Blue Water."

"A very sound theory," said Michael as Augustus and the two girls left the room. "Sounder still if Joss had been there."

"Precisely," said Digby, as the door closed, "so what I want to know is, who *did* pinch the thing? Offensive fella, I consider—but

Gussie being out of it, it must be one of us. Excuse my mentioning it, but me being out of it, it must be one of you two. Now unless you really want the damned thing, I say, *put it back*."

Michael's face was expressionless. "I'm thinking of bolting with it," he said.

"John going with his half too?"

"No," replied Michael. "I'm taking it all."

"Well," said Digby, looking at his watch, "could you go soon after lunch? I want to run up to town, and until the matter is cleared up Aunt seems to have other views."

"Do my best to oblige," said Michael.

AUNT PATRICIA DID NOT APPEAR at lunch, nor did Claudia. It was a painful meal, to me at any rate, though Digby seemed happy and Michael unconcerned. Afterward I went up to my bedroom, tired after my wakeful night, and threw myself on my bed.

I was awakened from a heavy sleep by the entrance of Digby a couple of hours later. He held a letter in his hand.

"Hi, hog," quoth he, "wake up and listen." He sat himself down on the foot of the bed.

"What's up now?" I yawned, rubbing my eyes.

"We've got to use our wits and do something to help Beau. He's done a bunk. Left this note with David. Says he pinched the Blue Water, and isn't going to face the police."

"*What?*" I cried.

"Read it," said Digby, and passed the letter to me.

My dear Dig, [it ran] When David gives you this, I shall be well on my way to—where I am going. Please tell Aunt there is no further need to chivvy any of you about the Blue Water. If a mystery merchant comes from Scotland Yard, tell him you knew I was in sore straights—or is it straits (or crookeds?)—for money, but that this is my first offense and I must have been led astray by bad companions (you and John). If I send you an address later, it will be in absolute confidence. I do hope that things will settle down quickly now. Sad, sad, sad! Give my love to Claudia.

Ever thine, Michael

"Impossible," I said.

"Of course it is, fathead," replied Digby. "He's off on the romantic tack. Taking the blame to shield his little brother."

"Which?" I asked. "You?"

"No."

"Me?"

"Subtle mathematician."

"But I didn't do it," I said. "You don't think Beau seriously supposes you or I would steal from Aunt Patricia, of all people?"

"Somebody has, haven't they?" said Digby. "Anyway, you seriously supposed that Beau had."

"How do you know?"

"By the way you looked at him—oh, half a dozen times."

"I had reason to suspect him."

"What reason—that you caught his wrist in the dark when, like you, he was probably only trying to catch Gussie in the act of putting it back?"

"I'd rather not say any more about it."

"Don't be an ass. The more we both know, the more we can help him. You needn't feel as though you were giving Beau away. I'm not asking you to tell Aunt or the police, am I, bunhead?"

This was true enough. No harm could result from Digby's knowing all that I knew. Therefore I told him about how I had met Beau in the drawing room last night with the key in his hand.

"And what were *you* doing, if one might ask?" interrupted my brother.

"Going to see if the Blue Water had been returned."

"Anyhow, *Beau* hadn't returned it, had he?" Digby grinned.

"No—but at the time I, naturally enough, thought he had," said I, "and I suppose that fixed the idea in my mind. I first got the idea when I caught his hand hovering over the glass cover in the darkness, but now that you have pointed out he was probably only doing what I was doing myself—"

"Exactly," said Digby. "Now, do you still suspect Beau?"

"Absolutely not."

"Very good then. Did *you* do it?"

"I did not."

"Nor did I."

A silence fell between us.

"I'm going dotty," said I at last.

"I've gone," said Digby, and we sat staring at each other for a long time.

DINNER THAT NIGHT was an extraordinary meal, at which only Isobel, Claudia, Augustus and I appeared. According to Burdon, Lady Brandon was dining in her own room; Mr. Michael was not in his room when David took up hot water; and Mr. Digby had been seen going down the drive soon after tea.

After dinner, I found myself alone in the drawing room with Isobel. She looked very lovely, I thought, with her misty blue eyes and her golden hair, fine as floss silk.

"Johnny," she said, coming toward me and laying her hands on my chest, "may I ask you a silly question? I know the answer, but I want to hear you say it."

"Certainly, dear."

"*Did you take the Blue Water?*"

"No, my dear, I did not," I replied, and drew her to me. She threw her arms round my neck and burst into tears. Lifting her up in my arms, I carried her to a sofa, covering her face with kisses. It had suddenly come upon me that I loved her—that I had always loved her. But hitherto it had been as a playmate; now it was as a woman. If this was a result of the Blue Water's theft, I was glad it had been stolen.

"Do you love me, darling Isobel?" I whispered, and for reply, she smiled through her tears and pressed her lips to mine. I thought my heart was stopping.

"*Love* you?" she asked. "I have loved you since I was a baby!"

"Don't cry," I said, ashamed of my inability to be articulate.

"I'm crying for joy," she sobbed. "Now that you have told *me* you didn't do it, I know you didn't. Of course, I never thought you did, only it was you Michael caught against the table; and I saw you go down in the night—to put it back, I thought."

51

"Saw me?" I asked, in surprise.

"I was awake and saw a light go by under my door. I came out and looked over the banisters."

"I went to see if the wretched thing had come back," I said. "And it was I who caught Michael when the lights were out. We were both expecting to catch Gussie."

"Oh, I have been so wretchedly unhappy," she said, "thinking appearances were against you. But I don't care now. Nothing on earth matters. So long as you love me . . ."

The sound of footsteps and a hand on the door brought us back to earth. We sprang to our feet, and when David entered, Isobel was sorting out some music at the piano and I was consulting a book with terrific abstraction from my surroundings.

"Might I speak to you, sir?" said David.

"You're doing it, David."

"In private, sir, a moment."

I went into the hall with him, and there he produced a note.

"Mr. Digby, sir, instructed me to give you this in private."

"Thank you, David." I went along to the smoking room, opening the letter as I went. Although I felt that I ought to be filled with apprehension, I could have danced down the corridor—to the disapproval of the various stately Brandons who looked down from its walls. "Isobel! Isobel!" sang my heart.

The smoking room was empty, and the click of balls from the neighboring billiard room told why. Gussie was at his favorite aimless employment.

I turned up the lights, poked the fire, pulled up the deepest chair, filled my pipe and lit it. Nothing seemed of much importance, compared with the fact of which my heart was chanting. Love is very selfish, I fear.

Then I read poor Digby's letter:

My dear John,

After terrific mental wrestling, which cost me a trouser button, I have come to the conclusion that I cannot let the innocent suffer for my guilty sin, or sinny guilt. By the time you get this, I shall

be well on my way to—where I am going. Tell Aunt I shall write
to her from town.

When you find yourself on the witness stand, tell the Beak that
you have always known me to be weak but not vicious, and that
my downfall was due to smoking cigarettes and going in for newspaper competitions. Also that you are sure I shall redeem myself
by hard work, earn thirty shillings a week, and return the thirty
thousand pounds out of my savings.

Write and let me know how things go on, as soon as I send
you an address—which you will, of course, keep to yourself. And
don't forget, directly you hear from Beau, let him know that I
have confessed and bolted, and that he can return to Brandon
Abbas. Give my love to Isobel.

Ever thine, Digby

For a moment this drove even Isobel from my mind. It had
never occurred to me that Digby would also flee. Did he, thinking
that Michael was guilty, flee to divert suspicion and divide the
pursuit? No, more likely, his idea was to help shield the person
whom Michael thought he was shielding—obviously either Claudia,
Isobel or me.

Suddenly it dawned on me that it was also *my* affair to help
prevent suspicion falling upon the two girls; that if my two
brothers could wreck their lives in such a cause, then so could I.
If I fled as well, the obvious solution for the detectives would
be that the theft was the result of a collusion among the three
rascally Geste brothers. But where should I go? Should I say
anything to Isobel?

One of these problems was subconsciously solved. From the
moment that I had learned of Michael's flight, I had had vague
memories of how, as children, we had sat at the feet of a young
French officer who had thrilled us with dramatic tales of a romantic-
sounding corps called the French Foreign Legion. At the end,
Michael had said, "I shall join the French Foreign Legion when
I leave Eton, get a commission and go into his regiment." Digby
and I had applauded the plan.

Had Michael remembered this, and was he now on his way to

win renown under a nom de guerre? . . . It would be so like Michael. And Digby? Had he had the same idea and followed him? It would be so like Digby. And I? Should I follow my brothers' lead, asking nothing better than to win their approval? It would be so like me.

Three romantic young asses! I can smile at them now. Asses, without doubt; but still with the imagination and soul to be romantic asses, thank God!

As COMPENSATION for a smaller share of my brothers' courage, I have been vouchsafed a larger measure of prudence—though some may think that still does not amount to much. I have met few men to equal Michael and Digby in beauty, strength and intelligence; but I, in spite of being an equally incurable romantic, was "longer headed" than they, and even more muscular. This is tremendous praise to award myself, but facts are facts.

Having decided to join them in disgrace, as well as in the flesh if I could, I began to consider ways and means. I can think better in the dark, so I knocked out my pipe, burned Digby's letter, and went up to bed.

The first fact to face, and it loomed most discouraging of all, was separation from Isobel in the very moment of finding her. Paradoxically, however, the exaltation over finding her gave me the power to leave her. It would be misery unspeakable—but what a beautiful misery for the heart of youth to hug to itself! Also I knew that it was useless for such children—she nineteen and I twenty, penniless and dependent—to think of marriage. Love was all and love was enough, until I should return, bronzed and dec-orated, a distinguished Soldier of Fortune, to claim her hand.

Should I tell her what I was going to do and have one last beautifully terrible hour with her in my arms, or should I write a letter to be given to her after I had gone? I am glad to say that I had the grace to decide according to what I thought better for her. In short, my choice was to write, and avoid embracing her as if I were going to the scaffold.

The next thing to consider was the problem of procedure. I

would breakfast with the others, and quietly walk off to catch the ten forty to Exeter. Then I would take the eleven forty-five thence to London. I had enough money to get that far.

However, I should want more money and sufficient kit to enable me to get to France and subsist for a few days in Paris. My watch, cuff links, cigarette case, and my good gold pencil would provide ample funds. I would arrive in France the next evening, sleep at a hotel and, as soon as possible, become a soldier of France.

Whatever my brothers had done, I should at least have followed their example worthily. And if Michael and Digby were there when I arrived—why, I should regret nothing but the separation from Isobel—a separation during which I would qualify for the honor of becoming her husband.

I think I had arrived at the position of Grand Commander of the Legion of Honor when I fell asleep.

I AWOKE IN THE MORNING in a very different frame of mind from that of the morning before. My heart was full of love, my brain full of schemes, and my whole being tingled with a sense of high adventure. When David brought my hot water, with his inevitable "Half past seven, sir, and a fine morning" (when the rain stops, or the fog clears, as the case might be), I told him I should give him a letter after breakfast, which he was to give to Miss Rivers after eleven o'clock.

Then I dressed, put my brushes, silk pajamas and shaving tackle into an attaché case, crammed in a shirt and socks, and went down to the smoking room. After some unsatisfactory efforts, I wrote to Isobel:

My darling beautiful Sweetheart,
　　Digby has bolted because he thinks Michael has shouldered the blame for this theft in order to protect the innocent and shield the guilty person (whoever he is). You'll be the first to agree that I can't sit at home and let both Digby and Michael do this. I should have had to leave you in a little while anyway to go back to Oxford, and that would have been an eight weeks' separation. As it is, we are only going to be parted until this silly business is

cleared up. I expect the thief will return the thing as soon as he finds that we three are all pretending we did it, and that we will not resume our ordinary lives until restitution is made.

I'll send you an address later on—but, just at first, I want you to have no idea where I am, and to say so. Aunt will go to the police, of course, and they will soon be on our track. But at least they will trouble no one at Brandon Abbas.

And now, darling Isobel, darling Faithful Hound, I am not going to try to tell you how much I love you—I am going to do it before you get this. Since last night, life has become a perfectly glorious thing. Nothing matters, because Isobel loves me and I love Isobel—for ever and ever.

Your devoted, adoring, grateful

Sweetheart

This honest, if boyish, effusion I gave to David, and repeated my instructions. He kept his face correctly expressionless, though he must have wondered how many more were going to give him epistles to be delivered after their departure to other members of the household.

Leaving the smoking room, I met Burdon in the corridor.

"Can you tell me where Mr. Michael is, sir?" he asked. "Her ladyship wishes to see him."

"No," I replied. "I don't know."

"Mr. Digby's bed have not been slep' in either, sir. I did not know the gentlemen were going away."

"I suppose they're off on some jaunt or other," I said. "I hope they ask me to join them."

"Racing, p'r'aps, sir?" suggested Burdon sadly.

"Shocking," said I, and left him, looking waggish to the best of my ability.

There were only the four of us at breakfast. Isobel's face lit up as our glances met, and we telegraphed our love to each other.

"Where's Digby?" asked Augustus. "Burdon said he wasn't in last night."

"I know no more than you do," I said.

"Funny—isn't it?" he sneered.

"Most humorous."

"Perhaps Aunt will think so, too. First Michael and then Digby, after what she said about not leaving the house!"

"Ought to have consulted you first, Gussie," said Claudia.

"Looks as though they didn't want to consult the police, if you ask me," he snarled.

"We didn't ask you, Gussie," said Isobel, and so the miserable meal dragged through.

Toward the end of it, Burdon came in. "Her ladyship wishes to see Mr. Digby," he said to the circumambient air.

"Want a bit of doing, I should say," sniggered Augustus.

"He's not here, Burdon," said I, looking under the table.

"No, sir," replied Burdon gravely, and departed. But a few minutes later he returned.

"Her ladyship would like to see you in her boudoir, after breakfast, sir," said he to me.

"Thought so," remarked Augustus, as the door closed behind the butler.

As soon as Augustus and Claudia had left, I turned to Isobel. "Come out to the Bower a minute, darling," I said, and we scuttled off together. There I crushed her to my breast and kissed her lips, her cheeks and eyes, as though I could never have enough. "Will you love me forever?" I asked. "Whatever happens?"

She did not reply in words, but her answer was very satisfying.

"Aunt wants me," then said I, and bolted back to the house.

But I had no intention of seeing Aunt Patricia. Mine should be the more convincing role of the uneasy criminal, who, suddenly sent for, has not the courage to face the ordeal, and flees. Going to my room, I took my attaché case from the wardrobe, pocketed a photograph of Isobel, and went quietly down the service staircase into the outer hall. In a minute I was across the shrubbery and away from the house.

Twenty minutes' walking brought me to the station, where I booked to Exeter. Thus, with a bigger lump in my throat than I had ever known since I was a child, I set out on as eventful a journey as ever a man took.

I REMEMBER NOTHING of that horrible journey from Exeter to London. It passed as a bad dream, and I awoke from it in Waterloo Station. I found that London was a very large place, and myself a very small atom of human dust therein. Walking out from the station into the purlieus thereof, I knew that the first thing to do was to convert my disposable property into cash—a distasteful undertaking, but essential to further progress.

As I walked down a mean street toward Westminster Bridge, my eye fell upon a pawnbroker's shop. I entered it and left five minutes later, having been relieved of not only my watch, cuff links, cigarette case and gold pencil but also my attaché case, which contained everything I needed for the night. The five pounds that I received for all these possessions was half what I had expected for the watch alone.

Crossing Westminster Bridge, with a total of about ten pounds in my pocket and misery in my heart, I made my way to Trafalgar Square, sorely tempted by the smell of food as I passed various restaurants. It occurred to me that it would be cheaper to dine, sleep and breakfast at the same place, so, asking a passerby where I could find inexpensive lodging, I was directed to Bloomsbury.

I obeyed, and had dinner, bed and breakfast for a surprisingly small sum. But, after sleeping for the first time in my life without pajamas, I was glad to get away. Having been shaved and shampooed at a barber's in Oxford Street, I went on my way, feeling more my own man again, to Dover. There I boarded the cross-Channel steamer.

At Calais, the sight of a French soldier, a sentry near the Custom House, gave me a real thrill. Was I actually going to wear that uniform in a day or two? A kepi, baggy red breeches, and a long overcoat, buttoned back from the legs?

However, on arrival in Paris, I had no idea how to offer my services to France as a mercenary soldier, so the first thing to do was to find a roof and bed while I set about the quest.

We bared our heads, Michael solemnly uttered the beautiful words, "Ashes to ashes and dust to dust; if God won't have you the devil must," and, applying a match, shoved the ship out into the middle of the pond.

In a minute I was across the shrubbery and away from the house.

While I shook Michael's hand, Digby shook my other one, and while I shook Digby's hand Michael shook my head.

He dragged him from the ground and jerked him heavily into the embrasure.

The Arab swordsmen were rallying to the attack on foot, but our disciplined rush swept them back.

Suddenly, the man standing beside him cried out and pointed to the fort. . . .
Zinderneuf was on fire!

My knowledge of Paris hotels was confined to such as the Bristol and the Ambassadors, but I knew these to be expensive, and places at which I might meet acquaintances. On the other hand, I did not want to blunder into an obscure cheap hotel, a foreigner without luggage, and run the risk of a visit from an *agent de police*. Therefore I was struck by a whimsical idea. Why not seek advice from the police themselves?

Sauntering along the noisy, busy thoroughfare that passes the Gare du Nord, I looked out for a gendarme. Presently I saw one standing on an island in the middle of the road. He stood silent, heavily caped, oppressed by great responsibilities. Crossing to him, I raised my hat, and in my politest French (which was not bad, thanks to a French governess in our youth) asked him if he could direct me to a quiet hotel.

Moving his eyes, but not any other portion of his majestic person, he examined me from top to toe.

"Monsieur is English," he pronounced.

I acknowledged the truth of his statement.

"*Hôtel Normandie, rue de l'Échelle.*" Then the all-seeing official eye left me and sought among the traffic. A white-gloved hand was suddenly raised, and an open cab, driven by a many-caped gentleman who did not look like a teetotaler, approached.

"Normandie, rue de l'Échelle," said my gendarme, and gave me a military salute as I thanked him, raised my hat, and stepped into the carriage.

After a beautiful drive through Paris, my heart sank as the cab drew up before a fashionable-looking hotel at a busy corner close to the rue de Rivoli. It looked expensive.

Trying to appear unconcerned, I entered the hall, received the bow of an imposing porter, and marched straight past the grand staircase to the office, where a pretty girl was talking to an American in American. This was good luck. I could make a much more convincing show in English than in French. Standing near, I waited for the American to go. Meanwhile, it was impossible to avoid hearing what the square-shouldered gentleman was saying.

When at length he took his key and went, I turned to the girl.

She seemed to be chewing a cud of sweet recollection and Mangle's Magnificent Masticating Gum.

"So you were raised in Baltimore!" I cried. "Prettiest girls and best cakes in America!"

"My!" said the young lady, smiling. "You know Baltimore?"

"*Know Baltimore!*" said I, and left it at that. "Lots of Americans and English here, I suppose, since the hotel folk are lucky enough to have you in the office? I suppose you speak French as well as any Parisian."

"Yes," she said. "Almost as well as I speak English. And there are a lot of Americans and Britishers here."

"Fine," said I. "I want to turn in for a day or two, just to sleep and breakfast. All upset at my place." (Very true, indeed.) "Got a room?"

"Sure," said my fair friend, and glanced at an indicator. "Fourteen francs. Going up now?" She unhooked a key and handed it to me. "*Deux cents vingt-deux*. The bellhop will show you."

"Not bringing any luggage," I said, and drew my entire fortune from my pocket, as one who would pay in advance.

"Shucks," she said, and from this I gathered that I was deemed trustworthy.

In the big book I wrote myself down as "Smith," but clung to the John, that there might be something stable in my dissolving universe. Then, with a bow and my best smile, I turned to the lift.

The lift boy piloted me to number two hundred and twenty-two, where, safe inside, I bolted the door and drew breath.

"*J'y suis, j'y reste,*" said I, in tribute to my French surroundings.

Relaxing in a big chair, I thought long thoughts of Isobel, my brothers, and Brandon Abbas; and I wondered what would happen tomorrow when I went to enlist in the Foreign Legion.

Were I a romancer as well as a romantic, I would now announce the dramatic entry of the French officer who had fired our young imaginations years before. He would enter the hotel and call for coffee and a cognac. I should go up to him and say, "*Monsieur le Capitaine* does not remember me, perhaps?" He would take my hand and say, "Mon Dieu! The young Englishman of Brandon

Abbas!" I should tell him of my ambition to be a soldier of France, and he would say, "Come with me, and all will be well. . . ."

Unfortunately no such meeting took place, and presently I crept unwillingly to bed. I fell asleep trying to remember his name.

THE NEXT DAY WAS SUNDAY, and I spent it miserably between the lounge and my bedroom. But on Monday morning, after an unsatisfying petit déjeuner, I again put myself in the hands of a barber, and, while enjoying his deft ministrations, had a bright idea. I would pump this chatty person.

"You don't know Algeria, I suppose?" I asked.

"But no, monsieur," he replied. "Is monsieur going there?"

"I hope to," I said. "A magnificent colony of your great country, that."

Ah, monsieur might well say so. Growing too, always growing, this excellent *pénétration pacifique* to the south.

"They do the pacific penetration by means of the bayonets of the Foreign Legion, don't they?" I asked.

The Frenchman smiled and shrugged. "A set of German rascals. But they have their uses. . . ."

"How do you get them?" I asked.

He explained that they just enlist at the head recruiting office of the French army in the rue Saint-Dominique. Then they were packed off to Africa. I let him talk, keeping the words "rue Saint-Dominique" clearly in my mind. The sooner I found this recruiting office the better, for funds would soon be running low.

On leaving the shop I hailed a fiacre, said, "Rue Saint-Dominique," and after a time I found we were in the military quarter of Paris. I saw the *École Militaire* and some cavalry barracks. The streets were thronged with men in uniform, and my heart beat higher as the cab turned from the Esplanade des Invalides into the rue Saint-Dominique. I thought perhaps it might not be good form to drive up in style to a recruiting office, so I paid the *cocher* and got out at the corner.

The rue Saint-Dominique was an uninspiring thoroughfare, narrow, gloomy, and very dingy. I soon came to a dirty little house

with a blue-lettered sign over the door: BUREAU DE RECRUTEMENT.
Below this was the laconic observation, ENGAGEMENTS VOLONTAIRES.

I opened the door and entered a long dark passage. On the wall
was a big placard which, in the names of Liberty, Equality and
Fraternity, offered to accept for five years the services of any ap-
plicant to *La Légion étrangère* (provided he was between the ages
of eighteen and forty), and to give him a wage of a sou, that's to
say about a halfpenny, a day. There seemed to me to be little of
Liberty, Equality or Fraternity about this proposal.

Venturing on, I came to a kind of ticket window, above which
were repeated the words ENGAGEMENTS VOLONTAIRES. I looked in
and beheld an austere person in uniform busily writing at a table.
The two gold stripes above his cuff inclined me to suppose that
he was a noncommissioned officer, though of what rank I knew
not. He ignored me and all other insects.

I coughed apologetically. I coughed appealingly. I coughed
upbraidingly, suggestively, authoritatively, meekly, hopefully and
quite hopelessly. "Monsieur le Capitaine," I murmured at last.

The man looked up. I liked him better when looking down.

"Monsieur would appear to have throat trouble," he observed.

"And monsieur ear trouble," I replied, in my young folly.

"What is monsieur's business?" he inquired sharply.

"I wish to join the *Légion étrangère*."

The man smiled, a little unpleasantly, I thought. "*Eh, bien.*
Doubtless monsieur will have much amusement at the expense of
the Sergeant Major there, too."

"Is monsieur only a Sergeant Major then?" I inquired.

"I am a Sergeant Major, and let me tell monsieur, it is the most
important rank in the French army. Wait by that door, please."
He indicated one marked COMMANDANT DE RECRUTEMENT.

I waited. I think I waited an hour.

Just as I was contemplating another visit to the ticket window,
the door opened and my friend, or enemy, appeared.

"Be pleased to enter, monsieur," said the Sergeant Major suavely,
and I for some reason bethought me of a poem from childhood,
"The Spider and the Fly," as I entered a large, bare orderly room.

It was no spider that I encountered, but a courtly Frenchman. He was a handsome, white-mustached man, dressed in a close-fitting black tunic and baggy red overalls with a broad black stripe. His cuffs were adorned with bands of gold and silver braid, and his sleeves with the five *galons* of a colonel.

"A recruit for the Legion, mon Commandant," said the Sergeant Major, and stood stiffly at attention.

The Colonel looked up from his desk as, entering, I bared my head and bowed. He rose with a friendly smile and extended his hand. Not thus, thought I, do British colonels welcome recruits.

"And you too wish to enlist in our Foreign Legion, do you?" he said as we shook hands. "Has England started an export trade in young men? You are the third Englishman this week!"

My heart gave a bound of joy. "Anything like me, sir?"

"*Au bout des ongles,*" was the reply. "Were they your brothers by any chance? But I will ask no indiscreet questions. Do you understand what you are doing, monsieur?"

"I have read the placard outside."

"It is not quite all set forth there." He smiled. "The life is a hard one. I would urge no one to adopt it, unless he were actually desirous of a life of discipline and hardship."

No, this certainly was not a case of the spider and the fly. Or it was an entirely new one, wherein the spider discouraged flies from entering the web.

"I wish to join, sir," I said. "I have heard something of the life from an officer of Spahis I once knew."

The Colonel smiled again. "Ah, *mon enfant*, but you won't be an officer of Spahis except after many long, lean years."

"One realizes that one must begin at the bottom, mon Commandant," I replied.

"Well then," said the Colonel, "the *engagement volontaire* is for five years, and the pay is a sou a day. A Legionnaire can reenlist at the end of the five years, and again at the end of ten years. At the end of fifteen years he is eligible for a pension. A foreigner, on completion of five years' service, can be naturalized as a French subject. You understand all that, mon enfant?"

"Yes, mon Commandant."

"Mind, I say nothing of what is meant by the term 'service' in the Legion. It is not all pure soldiering. Nor do I say anything as to the number of men who survive to claim the pension."

"I am not thinking of the pension, mon Commandant," I replied; "nor of the pay, so much as of a soldier's life—fighting, adventure . . ."

"Ah, there is plenty of that," said the Colonel. "Some of our most famous generals have been in the Legion. If you have been an officer in the army of your own country, you can begin as a probationary corporal, and avoid the ranks altogether."

"Please accept me as a recruit, mon Commandant," said I.

"Ah, we'll see first what the doctor has to say about you—though there is little doubt about *that*, I should think." He smiled and pulled a form toward him. "What is your name?"

"John Smith," said I.

"Age?"

"Twenty-one years" (to be on the safe side).

"Very well. If you pass the doctor I shall see you again. *Au 'voir, monsieur*," and with a curt nod to the Sergeant Major, the Colonel resumed his writing.

The Sergeant Major opened the door with a suave, "This way, monsieur," and led me across the passage to a small closet.

"Remove *all* clothing, please," he said, and shut me in.

I obeyed and then submitted myself to the investigations of an undergrown but overnourished gentleman, from beneath whose surgical smock appeared the baggy red trousers of the French army.

When he had finished with my vile body, he bade me replace it in the closet, clothe it, and remove it with all speed. This I did, and was reconducted into the Colonel's office.

"Well, mon enfant, you are accepted." The officer smiled.

"Can I enlist at once, sir?"

"Not until you have slept on it. Come back tomorrow, if you are still of the same mind, and I will enroll you. But think well; and remember, until you sign your name, you have committed yourself in no way whatsoever. Think well . . . think well. . . ."

Thanking him gratefully, I went from the room, hoping that all French officers were of this stamp, kindly and gentlemanly. My hope was not fulfilled.

In the corridor, the Sergeant Major observed, "I sincerely hope monsieur will return," and as I assured him that I would, I fancied, rightly or wrongly, that his smile was a little mocking.

EMERGING FROM THE GLOOM, I walked down the rue Saint-Dominique with a light, gay step. I could have danced, for I felt certain that Michael and Digby were but a day or two ahead of me, and that I might overtake them at any moment.

I spent the rest of my last day of freedom in sight-seeing and idleness. The next morning I paid my bill and departed from the Hôtel Normandie with a curious sense of escape.

Back at the *Bureau de Recrutement* I was shown into a waiting room by the same Sergeant Major, who observed, "Ah, monsieur has come back! Good!" and smiled unattractively.

In the waiting room were half a dozen fellow recruits. They were a mixed lot, apparently with nothing in common but poverty.

Before long, the Sergeant Major returned and bade me follow him to the Colonel's office.

"Ah, mon enfant," said the old soldier, as I entered and bowed, "so you have not thought better of it, eh?"

"I wish to enlist, mon Commandant," I said.

"Then read this form and sign it." He sighed. "Remember, though, that as soon as you have done so, you will be a soldier of France, amenable to martial law, and without appeal. Your friends cannot buy you out, and your consul cannot help you for five years. Nothing but death can remove you from the Legion."

I glanced over the gray printed form. Five years was a long time—but Isobel would only be twenty-four at the end of it. And if Michael and Digby had done it, so could I. It would be nice to return, a colonel at twenty-five, and take Isobel to my regiment. . . . I signed my name.

The Colonel smiled on reading my signature. "A little error, mon enfant?" he said. "Or you prefer this nom de guerre?"

I had written "J. Geste"!

Blushing, I asked to be allowed to change my mind, and the kindly old gentleman, tearing up the form, gave me another which I signed "John Smith."

"Now, my boy, listen to me," said he. "You are a duly enlisted soldier of France and must join your regiment at once. You are to catch the Marseille train from the Gare de Lyon this evening and report at the other end to Fort Saint-Jean." He rose and extended his hand. "I wish you good luck and quick promotion, mon enfant."

I thanked him and turned to commence my ride along the Path of Glory.

"Come with me, recruit," said the Sergeant Major, as he closed the door, "and move smartly."

In his office, he made out a railway warrant for Marseille, and a form that proclaimed the bearer to be a soldier of the Legion proceeding to Algeria. He then unlocked a drawer and doled out three francs. "Subsistence money, recruit," said he. "A squandering of public funds. Three sous would be ample."

I put another two francs on the table. "Let us part friends, Sergeant Major," said I, for I hate leaving ill feeling behind me if I can avoid it.

"Recruit," replied he, pocketing the money, "you will get on only if you respect all sergeant majors. Good-by."

THE FOLLOWING DAY, on arrival at the terminus of Marseille, I sauntered out into the busy, sunny streets. Feeling that Michael and Digby must be here as well cheered me up tremendously. But by the time I reached my destination my head was beginning to ache with the heat and hustle.

The medieval fort on the water's edge looked obsolete and dilapidated, with an ancient lighthouse tower and a drawbridge leading over a moat. The Sergeant of the Guard at the gate—I half expected to see him in breastplate, with trunk hose—ordered me to follow him along prisonlike stone corridors, damp and very depressing. He opened a door, jerked his thumb in the direction of the interior, and shut the door behind me.

I was in my first French barrack room.

Round the walls stood a score of cots and a number of benches on which lounged an assortment of men in civilian clothes— clothes ranging from lounge suits to rags. Michael and Digby were not among them and I felt a bitter disappointment.

The recruits looked at me, but though conscious of their regard, I was much more conscious of the foul atmosphere of the room. Every window was shut, and every man (as well as the charcoal stove) seemed to be smoking. Instinctively, I turned to the nearest window and wrestled it open.

To judge by the consternation evoked by my action, this was the first time a window had ever been opened in Fort Saint-Jean. At a table, three or four men who were playing cards cried out with great surprise and resentment. Ignoring them, I seated myself on the cot nearest the open window.

"Like the ceiling raised any?" inquired a drawling voice behind me in English.

Turning, I regarded the ceiling.

"No," I said, "it will do," and studied the speaker.

He was lying on the next cot, a small, clean-shaven man with a prominent nose, steel-trap mouth, and a look of great determination. His eyes were light gray, penetrating, his hair straw-colored and his face tanned.

"How did you know I was English?" I asked.

"What else?" he replied. "Pink and white . . . Own the earth . . . 'Haw! Who's this low fellah? Don't know him, do I?' . . . Dude . . . 'Open all the windahs now I've come!' . . . British!"

I laughed. "Are you American?"

"Why?"

"What else?" I drawled. "Don't care who owns the earth . . . Contempt for the effete English . . . Tar and feathers, Stars and Stripes. . . . 'I come from God's Own Country and I guess it licks Creation.' . . . Uneasy self-assertion. . . ."

The American smiled. (I never heard him laugh.) "Bo," said he, turning to the next cot, "here's a Britisher insulting of our country. Fierce, ain't it?"

A huge man slowly raised his head, ceased chewing, and regarded me solemnly. He then "fainted" with a heartrending groan.

"Killed my pard, you hev," said the little man. "He's got a weak heart." His friend had recovered sufficiently to continue his mastication either of tobacco or chewing gum. Lying there, he appeared to be some seven feet in length, four in breadth and two in depth. But in face he resembled the small man: same jutting chin and prominent nose. He looked a very bad enemy. Conversely, though, I gained the impression that he might be a very good friend. Indeed, I liked the look of them both, despite the fact that I seemed to fill them with amused contempt.

"Sez you suffers from oneasy self-insertion, Hank," went on the little man.

"Ain't inserted nawthen today, Buddy," replied the giant mildly. "I could insert a whole hog right now, and never notice it."

"Means well," said the other, "but he ain't et nawthen excep' cigarette ends for four days, an' he ain't at his best."

I stared. Certainly they looked haggard enough to be starving. I had felt bad after missing a single meal.

"Would you gentlemen have a drink with me?" I asked. "Brothers-in-arms and all that . . ."

Two solemn faces regarded me.

"Gee!" said Hank, and they rose as one man.

"Put it there, son," said the big man, extending the largest hand I had ever seen. The crushing match that ensued was painful.

"Where can we get something?" I asked, and Buddy said there was certain to be a canteen about. He had never heard of a base where a thirsty soldier with money was not encouraged to get rid of it.

"I can't drink till I've et," said Hank. "If I drinks on an empty stummick, I gets onreasonable."

At that moment, two soldiers entered carrying a long board with a row of tin bowls. Together they bawled, "*Soupe!*"

It was invitation enough. In a moment Hank was on his bed, a bowl in either hand. Buddy followed his example.

I looked round. There appeared to be more bowls than people, so

I snatched two before the hungry rush arrived from other parts of the room. My greed may be condoned as it was not in my own interest. I was not hungry. By the time I reached my cot, Hank had emptied one bowl and was rapidly emptying the other. When he had finished, I offered him one of mine.

"Honest Injun?" he asked doubtfully, but extending his hand.

"Had a big breakfast an hour ago. I got this for you and Mr.—er . . ."

"Buddy," said the little man and took the other bowl.

Hank swallowed his third portion. "You're shore swell, pard," he said.

"Blowed-in-the-glass," agreed Buddy, and I felt I had two friends.

A large German lumbered up, gesticulating. "You eat dree!" he shouted at Hank. "I only eat vun! You dirdy tief!"

"Sure thing, Dutchy," said Buddy. "Make him put it back."

The German shook a useful-looking fist under Hank's nose.

"I cain't put it back, Dutch," said Hank mildly. But finally, as the German waxed more aggressive, he laid his huge, soupy hand upon the fat face and pushed. The German staggered and sat down, looking infinitely surprised.

"*Now*, pard," said Hank to me, "I could look upon some wine without no evil effecks," and we trooped out.

The big quadrangle of Fort Saint-Jean was crowded with soldiers of every regiment. The place was evidently the clearinghouse for all soldiers coming from or returning to Africa. For the first time, I saw the Spahis of whom the French officer had talked. Their trousers were voluminous. They wore sashes that appeared to be yards in length and feet in width. In these they rolled each other up, one man holding the end while the other spun toward him. Gaudy waistcoats, Zouave jackets, fezzes, and vast scarlet cloaks completed their costumes.

Following a current of men toward a suggestive-looking squad of wine casks outside an open door, we found ourselves in the canteen. We made our way to the counter, where everybody was drinking cheap claret. "Drinks are on you, pard. Set 'em up," said Buddy.

"Gotta get used to wine with the other de*priv*ations," sighed Hank. And he drained the tumbler I had filled.

"Yep," said Buddy, "guess they don't allow no hard likkers in these furrin canteens."

"Set 'em up again," remarked Hank, and I procured them a second bottle. Turning away, I observed the noisy throng around me. They were a devil-may-care, tough-looking crowd, and I found myself looking forward to being in uniform and one of them.

As I watched, I saw a civilian coming toward us. I had noticed him in the barrack room. Although dressed in a shabby blue suit and burst shoes, he looked like a soldier. His face was bronzed, disciplined, and of a likeness to those around.

"Recruits for the Legion?" he said pleasantly, with only the slightest foreign accent. "Would you care to exchange information for a bottle?" He wore an ingratiating smile which did not extend to his eyes.

"I should be delighted," I replied, and put a two-franc piece on the counter.

He chose to think that the money was for him, and not for the man behind the bar. "You are a true comrade," he said, "and will make a fine Legionnaire. Ask me anything you want to know," and he included the two stolid Americans in a graceful bow. He was evidently a cultured person, but not English.

Said Hank, "I wants ter know when we gits our next eats."

"An' if we can go out and git some likker," asked Buddy.

"You'll get soup, bread and coffee at about four o'clock. You won't be allowed to leave here for any purpose until you are marched to the boat for Oran," was the reply.

"When will that be?" I asked.

"Tomorrow, by the steam packet, unless there is a troopship going the day after. They ship Legion recruits in—ah—dribbles? Dribblings? Driblets? Yes, driblets—by every boat that goes."

"Suppose a friend of mine joined a day or two before me," I asked, "where would he be now?"

"He is at Fort Sainte-Thérèse at Oran. He may go to Sidi-bel-Abbès tomorrow or the next day."

"Say, you're a walking encyclopedestrian," remarked Buddy, eyeing the man perhaps with more criticism than approval.

"I can tell you anything about the Legion," replied the man in his refined English. "I am an old Legionnaire, rejoining after five years' service and discharge."

"Speaks well for the Legion," I remarked cheerfully.

"Or ill for the chance of an ex-Legionnaire to get a crust of bread," he observed. "Tramped my feet off. Driven at last to choose between jail and the Legion. I chose the Legion, for some reason. Better the devils that you know than flee to the devils that you know not of. . . ."

"Guy seems depressed," said Hank.

"You speak wonderful English," I remarked.

"I do," was the reply; "but better Italian, Hindustani and French. My father was an Italian pastry cook in Bombay. I went to an English school there, run by the Jesuits. Talked Hindustani to my ayah. Got my French in the Legion, of course."

Then I blundered by saying, "Why did you join the Legion?"

"For the same reason *you* did. For my health," was the sharp reply, accompanied by a cold stare.

I had done that which is not done.

"And did you find it—healthy?" inquired Buddy.

"Not so much healthy as hellish."

We plied him with questions, and learned much that was useful and more that was disturbing. We gathered that the gentleman was known as Francesco Boldini. I came to the conclusion that I did not like him extraordinarily much; but that in view of his previous experience he would be a useful guide. When we returned to the barrack room, I formally retained him in that capacity with the gift of ten francs and the promise of such future financial assistance as I could give and he should deserve. "I am sorry I cannot spare more at present," said I, in unnecessary apology.

"Ten francs, my dear sir," he said, "is precisely two hundred days' pay to a Legionnaire. . . . Seven months' income. Think of it."

And I thought of it. I should need considerable promotion before being in a position to marry and live in comfort on my pay.

"DINNER" THAT EVENING consisted of soup, grayish bread, and black coffee. The soup was served in tin basins called gamelles. It seemed a kind of stew, quite nourishing. Afterward it was my privilege to entertain the whole band from the barrack room in the canteen.

Although I thoroughly enjoyed the evening, I noticed that Boldini waxed more voluble as he drank. If he could do anything else like a gentleman, he could not carry his wine like one. In fact, I liked him less and less as the evening wore on, and I liked him least when he climbed onto the counter and sang a vile song, devoid of humor. I admit, however, that it was very well received by the audience.

Back in our barracks, as I sat on my cot undressing, Buddy came over and whispered, "Got 'ny money left, pard?"

"Certainly," I replied. "You're welcome to . . ."

"Welcome nix. If you got 'ny money, shove it inside yer piller an' tie the end up."

"Hardly necessary, surely?" said I.

"Please yerself, pard," replied Buddy. He glanced meaningly at Boldini, who was lying fully dressed on his cot.

"Oh, nonsense," said I, "he's not that bad."

Buddy shrugged and departed. I finished undressing, got into the dirty sheetless bed, put my money under my pillow, then lay awake for a long time, dreaming of Isobel, Brandon Abbas, and the Blue Water with its mysterious fate.

I was awakened in the morning by bugles. A corporal entered the room, bawled, *"Levez-vous donc!"* and departed.

I dressed, then felt beneath my pillow. My money was not there! I felt sick. . . .

"Here it is," said Buddy behind me. "Thought I'd better mind it when I aheered yore nose sighs. Shore enuff, about four a.m. this morning, over comes Mister Boldini to see how you wuz agettin' on. . . . 'All right, bo,' sez I, speakin' innercent in me slumbers, 'I'm amindin' of it,' I sez. An' Mister Boldini sez, 'Oh, I thought somebody might try to rob him.' 'So did I,' I sez, 'and I was right,' an' the skunk scoots back to his hole."

"Thanks, Buddy," I said, feeling foolish.

"I tried to put you wise," he said. "Now you know."

That afternoon we assembled in the courtyard, formed in fours, and marched to the *bassin*, where a steamer awaited us. We were herded onto this aged packet for a miserable three-day voyage.

CHAPTER 4: ARRIVAL IN AFRICA

IT WAS EARLY in the morning when we reached Oran. A sergeant came on board, called roll, then marched us ashore.

I am in Africa! said I to myself, as down a wide street of flat-roofed houses we marched, stared at by half-naked Negroes, burnous-clad Arabs, French soldiers and European civilians. On through narrow slums and alleys we went, till at length the town was behind us and the desert in front.

For an hour or more we marched by road across the desert, until we came in sight of an old building, another obsolete fort, which Boldini said was Fort Sainte-Thérèse—our destination.

In the courtyard of this barrack hostelry roll was again called, and then we followed our sergeant to a barrack room. As I went in, a well-known voice remarked, "Enter the Third Robber."

It was Digby's!

Michael and Digby were sitting on a bench, hands in their pockets, pipes in their mouths, and consternation upon their faces.

"Good God!" exclaimed Michael. "You unutterable fool!"

I fell upon them. While I shook Michael's hand, Digby shook my other one, and while I shook Digby's hand, Michael shook my head. They then threw me upon the bed and we all fell in a heap.

Then we realized that we were objects of interest to the others, particularly Boldini. "Third *robber!*" he muttered to a German, called Glock.

"Beau and Dig," said I, "let me introduce two shore-enough pardners from God's Own Country—Hank and Buddy. . . . My brothers, Michael and Digby."

They laughed and held out their hands.

73

"Americans possibly," said Digby.

"Shake," said Hank and Buddy as one.

"Mr. Francesco Boldini," said I. "My brothers." But neither Michael nor Digby offered his hand until Boldini reached for it.

"I think wine is indicated, gentlemen," he said and, eyeing us, added, "'when we three robbers meet again,' so to speak."

Michael invited Hank and Buddy to join us, and Boldini led the way to the canteen, where the three of us sat, drinking little and watching the others drink a good deal—for which Michael insisted on paying.

Boldini told us among other things that the African daily ration was half a pound of meat, three sous' worth of vegetable stew, a pound and a half of bread, half an ounce of coffee and half an ounce of sugar. He said it was nourishing but deadly monotonous. "Still, one gets used to it, just as one gets used to washing with soap and water," he said. "Or do you fine gentlemen wash with champagne and a slice of cake?"

It struck me that Boldini was a man who would need keeping in his place. At the same time, I was glad to see that Beau and Digby seemed to like Hank and Buddy as much as I did. Of the other recruits, only one struck me as interesting. He was well dressed and well spoken, probably an ex-officer of the French or Belgian army. He had "soldier" stamped all over him. He called himself Jean Saint-André, but I suspected a third name, with a *de* in front of it. He had rather attached himself to us three, and we all liked him.

Toward evening, Beau proposed that we brothers should spend a minimum of time in our loathsome barrack room (its sole furniture being a great wooden guard bed, innocent of mattress, on which a score of men were expected to lie side by side). Digby observed that the air in the courtyard would be much cleaner. So we selected an eligible corner, seated ourselves in a row against the wall, and prepared for a night under African stars.

"Well, my idiotic pup, what do you think you're doing here?" began Michael, as soon as we were settled and our pipes alight.

"Fleeing from justice," said I.

"Did you bring the Blue Water with you?" asked Digby.

"No."

"Careless," said Michael. "But bring us up to date on things. How's everybody bearing up?"

I told them the details of my evasion, and of the respective attitudes of Augustus, Claudia and Isobel. "It's rough on Aunt Patricia," I concluded.

"Thirty thousand pounds," mused Digby. "Uncle Hector will go mad and bite her when he finds out."

"Doesn't bear thinking of," said I.

In the silence that followed, I was aware of a sound close beside us where a buttress of the wall projected. Probably a rat or some nocturnal bird; possibly a dog.

"When are we going to let them know we're in the Legion?" I asked at last.

"Why let them know at all?" said Michael. "Runaway criminals don't write home."

"But, Beau," I objected, "how are they to let us know if the stone turns up if they don't know where we are?"

"True," agreed Michael. "At least we ought to let Aunt Patricia know we're hale and hearty, but without telling her that we're all together. We don't want some fool saying that we agreed to share the blame while the thief is still at Brandon Abbas."

"Who *is* the thief?" said Digby.

"I am," said Michael.

"Then why the devil don't you put it back?"

"Too late now. Besides, I want to lie low, then sell it for thirty thousand pounds five years hence. I'll invest the money and have the income for life. Live like Uncle Hector."

"On Uncle Hector's money?" I said.

"Doubles the joy of it, what?" replied Michael.

"Funny thing," put in Digby, "that's just what I'm going to do. Except I find one can't get more than twenty thousand. I'm going to put it into a south-sea-island plantation, buy a schooner and be my own supercargo. Honolulu, ukuleles, surf riding . . ."

"What are you doing with the Blue Water meanwhile?" I asked, humoring the humorists.

"Always carry it about with me," said Digby. "If I get an eye knocked out I shall wear it in the empty socket. Blue-eyed boy. Good idea, that."

"Rotten idea," objected Michael. "Marsupial is the tip. Kangaroo's custom. They carry about their young and their money and things in a sort of bag . . . in front . . . accessible. I keep it on me night and day, wash-leather pouch in a money belt I bought in London. Diamond merchants always wear them when they travel. Round their little tummies under their vests."

And so we ragged and chatted, until toward morning we dozed, and the dawn found us cold and stiff, but quite happy. We were together; life, the world, and adventure before us.

A THIRD DRAFT OF RECRUITS arrived after morning soup, and we learned that all were to be evacuated that day to Sidi-bel-Abbès, depot of the First Regiment. As we were falling in to march to Oran Station, Boldini came up to my brothers and me. "Let's stick together, we four," he said. "I know the ropes at Sidi, can get you in right with the corporals. Sergeant Lejaune's a friend of mine."

"We brothers are certainly sticking together," said Michael.

At the station we entrained in a poor specimen of the West Algerian Railway Company that made its way to Sidi-bel-Abbès at an average rate of ten miles an hour. I remember being surprised that the African countryside mainly consisted of cultivated fields, orchards and gardens, and it was not until we were approaching our destination that sand hills and wildness prevailed.

We reached Sidi-bel-Abbès in the evening. Here we were lined up and marched off in fours along a broad road. As we marched, I got a somewhat Spanish impression of the outskirts of the town, probably because I heard the tinkling of a guitar and saw some women with high combs and mantillas. Entering the town itself through a gate in the huge ramparts, we were in a curiously hybrid atmosphere in which moved stately Arabs, smart French ladies, omnibuses, camels, men and women straight from the Bible, and others straight from the boulevards. No less hybrid was the architecture. The eye passed from white mosque to gaudy café, from

Moorish domes to French newspaper kiosks, and from Eastern bazaars to Western hotels.

Turning from a main thoroughfare, we entered a lane between the barracks of the Spahi cavalry and those of the Foreign Legion. Through the railings of great iron gates we could see a colossal yellow building at the far side of a parade ground.

A door was opened beside the gates and we filed through. A guard observed us without enthusiasm. The Sergeant of the Guard emerged from the guardhouse and looked us over, then closed his eyes while he slowly shook his head.

A knot of men, clad in white uniforms with wide blue sashes, gathered and regarded us.

"Mon Dieu!" said one. "That blackguard Boldini's back again!"

Boldini affected deafness.

Then appeared from the regimental offices the only man I have ever met who seemed to me to be wholly bad—evil all through. He was a fierce-looking, thickset man, glaring of eye, swarthily handsome, with the jowl of a bulldog. He also had the curious teeth-baring jaw thrust of a bulldog, and there were two deep lines between the heavy brows. This was the terrifying Color Sergeant Lejaune. To his superiors he was invaluable, to his subordinates unspeakable. Later, through a deserter from the Belgian Army, we learned that Lejaune had been dismissed from the Belgian Congo for atrocities exceeding even the limit fixed by good King Leopold's men. But now, in the Legion, he clearly had scope for his brutality.

Lejaune called the roll and looked us over. Noting the insignificant stature of Buddy, his face set in a sneer.

"An undersized cur," he remarked to the Sergeant of the Guard.

"Guess I've seen better things than you dead on flypaper, anyhow," replied Buddy, who did not mistake the contempt in the Sergeant's tone.

Mercifully Lejaune knew no English—but he knew that a recruit had dared to open his miserable mouth. He roared, "Silence, dog! Speak again and I'll kick your teeth down your throat."

Buddy did not understand a word, but he heard the angry roar, and he was too old a soldier not to stiffen to attention.

The mischief was done, however, and Buddy, and Buddy's friends, were marked men.

When Lejaune's eye fell upon Boldini it halted, and a long look passed between them. Neither spoke. In time it became clear to us that there was an old bond between the two men. Vaerren, the Belgian deserter, told us that Boldini had been a civilian subordinate in Lejaune's Congo district, and had been imprisoned for falsifying his trade returns. Of the truth of this I know nothing, but I do know that Lejaune favored Boldini, and later, when he himself became Sergeant Major, he procured Boldini's promotion to corporal.

Next, Lejaune looked at us Gestes.

"Runaway pimps," he said. "Show me your hands."

We held them out. "Going to tell our fortunes. . . . Beware of a dark ugly man," whispered Digby to me.

"Never done a stroke of work in your lives," said Lejaune. "I'll manicure you before you die, by God."

He looked Hank over. "A lazy hulk," he observed. "I'll teach you to move quickly, in a way that'll surprise you."

"Shore, bo," replied Hank, ignorant of what had been said.

"Quiet, you chattering ape! Speak again and I'll cripple you for life!" Hank also grasped that silence was golden.

Having duly impressed the draft, Color Sergeant Lejaune announced that the Seventh Company would be afflicted with the lot of us. He then roared, *"Garde à vous! Pour defiler! Par files de quatre, à droite . . . En avant. . . . Marche!"*

We marched to the storeroom and received our kit, which, in addition to two cloth uniforms, included white fatigue uniforms, underclothing, blue sashes and boots, but no socks, for the Legion does not wear them. We were then inspected by a noncom called an *adjudant-major*, and marched to our caserns, or barrack rooms.

Ten of us (Boldini, Saint-André, Buddy, Hank, Glock, two newcomers called Vogué and Maris, and we brothers) were directed to a huge, clean chamber in which were thirty beds. Here we were then handed over to some Legionnaires, who were polishing their belts and accouterments.

"Recruits for you," said Corporal Dupré. "Show them what to do. Kit, bedding, everything." And he left the room.

"Name of a Name of a Name!" gabbled one of the men. "If it isn't old Boldini come back!" He roared with laughter.

"Wait till I'm a corporal, friend Brandt," said Boldini. "Meanwhile take five of the recruits and I'll attend to the others." Boldini proceeded to direct us to appropriate beds and put our kits on them. He then gave us an exhibition of clothes folding, and built up a neat little paquetage of uniform and kit on the shelf above his bed.

"There you are—do that first," said he. "Everything in elbow-to-fingertip lengths, piled so," and we set about folding our kits as he had done. Then we had a lesson in *astiquage*, the polishing of belts and cartridge pouches; and then in rifle cleaning.

THAT NIGHT, AFTER THE lights-out bugle, we completed our kit preparations for the morrow by the meager light of the casern night lamp. We gathered that we should be aroused at five fifteen in the morning, and should have to be on parade with everything immaculate at five thirty. So, with the fears of the novice, we recruits determined to have everything ready before we went to bed.

Michael's bed was in the corner by the window, Boldini's was next, Digby's next, then that of an Italian called Colonna. Mine came next, then Brandt's, then Buddy's, and so on—always an old Legionnaire next to a recruit. By the door was the bed of Corporal Dupré, who was in command of the escouade. Apparently he was an active, bustling person, not unkindly when sober; but when overfull of wine he was sullen and dangerous.

While we were putting the last touches to our kits and extracting advice from Boldini, he came into the room, undressed and went to bed. As he lay down he bawled, "Silence! If any man makes a sound, he'll make the next sound in hospital," and fell asleep.

We got into our beds in a silence that could be felt.

I was awakened by the *garde-chambre* shouting something as he lit the lamp that hung from the ceiling. Men sat up in bed. Each took a mug from a hook below the shelf above his head, and held it out as the garde-chambre went round with a great jug of coffee.

79

It was hot and strong. Next Corporal Dupré shouted, "Levez-vous!" and Michael, Digby and I rushed to the lavatory, dashed our heads into water and fled back, toweling.

In a short time we were dressed and ready, with our beds made and our kits laid out. The garde-chambre had swept up the dust, and Corporal Dupré had been round to see that everything was tidy. Then, following a shout of "Garde à vous," the Color Sergeant of the company entered to inspect. Remarkably, the great man's face remained impassive throughout his inspection. All was well.

We took our rifles from the rack, put our bayonets in their frogs, and clattered down to the parade ground. There the battalion was marched to field exercises, and the recruits were told off by escouades and taken out to a drill ground for physical training, which today was running. On other mornings it took the form of gymnastics, boxing or a long route march.

That first day set the pattern of our routine. On our return to the barracks, we had our morning meal of Legionnaire's soup and a quarter liter of wine. After a rest, we recruits had a lecture and drill, while the battalion did attack-formation exercise on the plateau. Then, having tidied up around the barracks, we were free to go to the lavabo to wash our uniforms. At five o'clock we got our second meal, exactly like the first, and were then finished for the day, save that we had to polish our arms and equipment. Yet here the poverty of the Legion helped us, for no man had to do a stroke while he had a halfpenny to spare. To our comrades a job meant the means of getting a pack of caporal cigarettes, a bottle of wine, or a piece of much needed soap. We three did not shirk our work, but often, when weary, we gave our astiquage to one of the many who begged to do it.

Aided by our intelligence, strength, sense of discipline and a genuine desire to make good, we three soon became good soldiers. More fortunate than most, we were well educated and had a little money. Less fortunate than most, we were accustomed to varied food, comfortable surroundings, leisure and, above all, privacy.

But at first, everything was new and romantic; we were together, and we were by no means unhappy. On our first Sunday morning in the Legion, we three sat on Michael's bed and held a Council of War, as we had often done at Brandon Abbas. Having learned from Boldini that the English police would not pursue a Legionnaire so long as he remained in the Legion, it was decided that I should write to Isobel, telling her where I was, that I knew where Michael and Digby were, and could send them any messages. Isobel was to use her discretion as to admitting that she knew where I was.

Michael and Digby approved my letter, but I privately inserted a message of undying love, which she could destroy should she decide to show the letter itself to Aunt Patricia.

A fortnight later, I got a private love letter that made me wildly happy, and with it a longer letter that I could send to Michael and Digby. This latter said that things were going on at Brandon Abbas exactly as before. Aunt Patricia had communicated neither with the police nor anybody else. Apparently she had accepted the fact that one of the Gestes had stolen the Blue Water, and, incredibly, was doing nothing about it—simply awaiting Uncle Hector's return.

"I cannot understand her," Isobel wrote. "She has told Gussie and Claudia and myself that we are free of suspicion, and she wishes us to make no further reference to the matter. Gussie is, of course, unbearable. He has 'known all along that you three would come to a bad end,' but while certain that you are all in it together, he believes that you, John, are the actual thief. I told him that I had a belief, too. I said, 'I believe that if you gave your whole soul to it, Gussie, you might someday be fit to clean John's boots.'

"I don't know *what* Uncle Hector will say about the delay in going to Scotland Yard. It almost looks as though Aunt wants the culprit to escape. I can't make it out *at all*. . . ."

Michael read this letter without comment.

"I wonder why Aunt Patricia hasn't called the police," I remarked at last.

"Yes," said Michael. "Funny, isn't it?"

Then, turning, I noticed that Boldini was asleep on his bed behind us. It was curious how quietly that man could move, with his catlike steps and silent ways.

As THE WEEKS PASSED, Boldini stuck to us closer than a brother sticketh, and after his first usefulness was over we certainly did not desire his society for himself alone. But apparently he desired ours, and ardently. The only times that we were not troubled by his presence was when Buddy was with us. The American would have none of him, and scrupled not to say so.

"Get to hell outa this, Boldini," he would say. "Go gnaw circles in the meadow and keep away from me with both feet. . . . Scoot!" Then he would turn to us and say, "Watch out, he's on your trail fer somethin'. He's Lejaune's spy."

Another person who was most certainly on our trail was Color Sergeant Lejaune himself—now, alas, Sergeant Major. We were far too careful, however, to give him the opportunity he desired. When he came in for inspection, he gave our kits and bedding a longer, more searching inspection than he gave anybody else's except Buddy's, and when I met the stare of his eyes, I thought of a panther whose sole mental content was hate.

"Our name's mud," said Buddy. "He makes me feel like I butted into a grizzly b'ar—on'y I liked the b'ar better."

It was also clear that Corporal Dupré had found that he had said the wrong thing when he told Lejaune that we were model recruits. Dupré was not a bad fellow at heart, but "he had got to live," and it grew clearer as the weeks went by that we three could do nothing right and Boldini nothing wrong. Our chief offense was that we would commit no offense—but we walked on very thin ice.

In less than a couple of months we became full-blown Legionnaires. Above the head of my bed appeared a card, bearing the legend JOHN SMITH, No. 18896, SOLDAT DEUXIÈME CLASSE. I was a second-class Soldier of Fortune. In time I should be a *soldat première classe*, if I were good.

Meanwhile, we now learned what marching really was, and why the Legion was known as the *cavalerie à pied*. Over sand and stones, under the African sun, and with our heavy kits, we would march for appalling distances at five kilometers an hour. On one occasion we took a stroll of five hundred miles, marching continuously at thirty miles a day.

In addition to these marches, we trained in skirmishing and scouting, drill, first aid, field engineering, target practice—and by the time we felt ourselves old soldiers, we also began to feel we were stagnating mentally. Our brains demanded exercise. Michael decreed that we should study Arabic, both for the good of our souls and for future usefulness when we should be generals entrusted with diplomatic missions or military governorships.

We got books from the library, engaged a half-caste clerk who worked in the *Bureau Arabe* to meet us four evenings a week for conversation, and took to haunting Arab cafés instead of French. We made rapid progress and, after a time, were speaking Arabic to each other.

Although we were wary of Lejaune, the Americans were not so careful. For one thing, they sometimes drank the filth sold in the low-class wineshops of the Spanish quarter. While the crude alcohol brewed from figs, rice or wood made Buddy's temper explosive, it rendered Hank indiscriminatingly affectionate and, singing joyously, apt to fall upon the neck of the Sergeant of the Guard when the latter admitted him at night. Then was Lejaune happy. When they were confined to barracks, he would have the defaulters' roll called at odd times, in the hope of their missing it. When they were in the *salle de police*, he would see that the guard turned them out hourly, under pretense of suspecting that they had tobacco or drink. Sometimes in the middle of the night he would go to their cells, arouse them with a roar, and give an order in the hope that it would be disobeyed through resentment or drunken stupidity. I think he would have given a month's pay to have goaded one of them into striking him, and it was my fear that Buddy would do so. However, they were old soldiers and wily Americans.

So the months passed, and every week I heard from my darling. Nothing happened at Brandon Abbas. Gussie had gone to Sandhurst, and Uncle Hector had postponed his homecoming to shoot bear in Kashmir. No reference was ever made to the Blue Water, no questions had been asked of Isobel, and she had volunteered no information about being in communication with me.

ONE EVENING, MARIS, A SWISS EX-COURIER who spoke English, came to me as I lay on my cot, and said, "Monsieur Smith, you have done me many a good turn. Will you and your brothers meet me at Mustapha's at six tonight? It will be worth your while. We shall be safe there, if we talk in English." He glanced apprehensively toward Colonna and an Italian named Guantaio, who were working together at a nearby table.

I thanked him and said that my brothers and I would be there.

Mustapha's was an Arab café where we could get splendid coffee very cheaply—thick and black, spiced with hashish oil, orange essence and other flavorings. Here we rested ourselves on a low divan with a solid wall behind us, and, as our little clay cups of coffee lay steaming on the floor in front of us, Maris began in his excellent English: "It's like this, my friends. Boldini is up to his old tricks again. Last night I was sitting in the Tlemcen Gardens. It was getting dark. Behind the seat were bushes, and a path ran by the other side. Some Legionnaires came along and sat down on a seat that must have been just behind the bushes. They were talking Italian. I know Italian well, and I listened. Boldini it was, and Colonna and Guantaio. He had been trying to get them to do something and they were afraid. Boldini also wanted Colonna to change beds with him, to make this something easier to do.

"'Yes, and what if I am caught?' said Colonna. 'What about his brothers, and his friends the Americans?'

"'And what about *your* friends,' said Boldini, 'me and Guantaio, Vogué and Gotto? *What about Sergeant Major Lejaune?* Aren't Lejaune and I like brothers?'

"'Why not do it yourself then?' said Guantaio.

"'Because I'm going to be made corporal soon, and I mustn't be in any rows. . . . Ah, when I'm corporal, I shall be able to look after my friends, eh?' He reminded them of what they could do with a thousand francs—more than fifty years' pay, for a two-minute job.

"Then Guantaio, who seems to be pluckier than Colonna, said, 'How do you know he has got it?'

"Boldini replied, 'Because I heard them say so. They are a gang. They have asked me if thieves in the Legion are given up to the police. When they joined each other at Oran, I guessed it from what they said, and the way they flashed their money. They got together at night out in the courtyard, and I crept up behind a buttress and listened. I could not hear everything, but they spoke of a jewel robbery and thirty thousand pounds. The one they call *le Beau* said he kept it like the *canguro* . . . the kangaroo . . . keeps its young! And where is that? In a pouch on its stomach. That is where this thief keeps his jewel. It's a thousand francs for the man that gets me the pouch. I'll take the risk of getting the jewel sold for more than a thousand. I could put the lamp out, and one man could gag and hold him while the other got it. Then they could run to their beds in the dark. . . .'

"And much more of the same sort he talked, egging them on, and then they went away, but with nothing settled," said Maris.

We burst into laughter at the mention of the kangaroo. Digby asked if Boldini had not also divulged that he wore a sapphire eye.

"The fool overheard an elaborate joke," explained Michael, "but we're much obliged to you."

"Oh, he is the fool all right," said Maris; "but he is also the knave. I just tell you because I like you English gentlemen, and they may try to steal your money."

We filled the worthy Maris up with pancakes and honey and strolled back to barracks.

When we were alone, I said to Michael, "You *do* wear a money belt, Beau. Let me have it at night for a bit—just in case."

"Why?"

"Well, you could favor these gentle Italians with your full personal attention if you had no property to protect. Also you could establish that you don't wear a money belt at night."

"I'd sooner establish despondency in the thief," said Michael.

"What a lark!" chuckled Digby. "I'm going to wear a brick under my sash and swear it's a ruby. Anyone that pinches it can have it for keeps. I must find this Boldini lad."

Although I did not say so, I did not regard the matter, like Digby, as a lark. It seemed to me that a man might well be found dead in his bed and nobody be any the wiser. However, I had underestimated the Legion's queer code of morals. One might steal any article of uniform or kit and be no thief. This was merely to "decorate oneself." But to steal private property was far from "decoration"; it was the ultimate crime, infinitely worse than murder. Such a thief was punished by the men themselves without appeal to authority. This was Legion law—a law I was soon to see in operation.

That very night in our barracks I was awakened by a crash and a shout. Springing up, I saw two men struggling on the floor near Michael's bed. The one on top, pinning the other down with a hand on his throat, was Michael. As I leaped from my bed, men were running with angry shouts to see what, and who, had broken their sacred sleep.

"Wring the sneakin' coyote's neck, bo," shouted Buddy, and with cries of "Thief! Thief!" a wave of gesticulating men swept over the two and bore one of them to the surface. It was neither Guantaio nor Colonna, neither Gotto nor Vogué. White-faced and imploring, in the grip of a dozen outraged Legionnaires, was a man from the next room.

I looked around for Boldini. He was sound asleep in his bed! And so was Corporal Dupré, with his face to the wall—both of them men whom the squeak of a mouse would awaken.

"What are you doing here, *scélérat?*" shouted half a score of fierce voices.

"What about it?" roared the huge bearded Schwartz, who had got the man by the throat, to my brother. "Was he stealing?"

"On the table with him!" yelled Brandt.

"Yes, crucify the swine," bawled Schwartz, and the crowd snarled. Several had bayonets in their hands.

"I lost my way," screamed the prisoner.

"And found it to the bed of a man who has money," laughed a voice. "Legion law! On the table with him!"

"Give the guy a fair trial!" shouted Hank, to no avail, and Michael jumped up on the table.

"Silence, you fools!" he shouted to the crowd. "Listen! I woke up and found the man feeling under my pillow. I thought he was somebody belonging to the room, somebody I have been waiting for. Well—he isn't. Let him go—he won't come again. . . ."

At that there was a yell of derision, and Michael was sent flying by a rush of angry men.

While he, Digby and I were struggling to get to the table, the thief was flung onto it and held down; a bayonet was driven through each of his hands and another through each of his ears.

Suddenly there was a cry of *"Guard!"* and a swift rush in all directions. The guard and a corporal tramped in, to find a silent room of sleeping men in the midst of which were we three, pulling bayonets out of a white wooden table and a whiter whimpering man.

"What's this?" said the Corporal. "An accident," he answered himself. Then turning to the guard, he gave the curt order: "To the hospital," and the guard carried the wretched creature away.

Whether he was incited by Boldini or was merely trying to rob a man known to have money, I did not know. When he came out of hospital, we learned that he was a Portuguese named Bolidar. He stuck to his absurd tale that he was feeling his way into what he thought was his own bed, and we concluded that he was either staunch to his confederates or afraid to implicate them.

As the old Legionnaires prophesied, we heard nothing from the authorities about the assault. Clearly it was considered best to let the men enforce their own laws, provided those laws were reasonable and in the public interest.

Within a week or two, however, we were the most famous gang of international jewel thieves in Europe, and had got away with a diamond worth over a million francs. Buddy solemnly informed me that Bolidar knew all this "for certain." Bolidar had got it from a friend. No names, but if Hank and Buddy could "rescue" the diamond, he, Bolidar, was in a position to promise them a thousand francs *and* the protection of—someone who was in a position to protect them.

"So there you are, pard," concluded Buddy, with an amused grin. And there we were.

But only for another month. At the end of that time we all found ourselves in a selected battalion, a thousand strong, under orders for the south. We were going to "demonstrate" there, and "demonstrating" meant further peaceful penetration with the bayonet, and chances of destruction and promotion.

CHAPTER 5: FORT ZINDERNEUF

WE LEFT SIDI-BEL-ABBÈS in the spirit in which boys leave school at the end of the half; for the escape from monotony was inexpressibly delightful. The bitterness in my cup of joy was the knowledge that, being constantly on the move, I could only hear from Isobel at long intervals. I poured out my heart in a long letter the night before we marched; told her I was certain I should see her again but begged her not to waste her youth thinking of me if a year passed without news, as I should be dead.

Having had my hour of self-pity, the next morning, with a hundred rounds of ammunition in my pouch, joy in my heart and a terrific load on my back, I marched out of the gates with the others to the music of our band playing "The March of the Legion."

After several days of marching and nights of camping in the desert, we reached Ain-Sefra, where we rested to recoup and refit. Here we learned that the whole Sahara was fermenting in one of its periodic states of unrest, with Tuareg raids on protected villages, tribal revolts, and sporadic outbursts of mutiny and murder. There was also much talk of big concentrations of Tuareg and other Arab tribesmen planning to strike simultaneously at every French outpost on the Saharan border from Morocco to Tripoli. Their program, in the name of Allah the All-merciful and Mahomet his Prophet, was to free the land of Islam from the polluting presence of us unbelieving dogs. To this end, Morocco, Tunisia, Tripoli and Egypt were to join hands under the banner of the Mahdi el Senussi.

From Ain-Sefra we marched to Douargala, where a large force of arms was concentrating, and from here we proceeded south. After endless desert marching, the battalion found itself strung out along a chain of oases between which communication was maintained by camel patrols that met halfway and exchanged reports, cigarettes and bad language.

It was at El Rasa, the last of these oases, that our half company first came in contact with the Arabs. Goumiers rode in at dawn one day with the news that they had seen the campfires of a big Tuareg *harka* about twenty miles to the south, where an ancient well marked the crossroads of two caravan routes as old as civilization.

We were in touch with the enemy at last. At any moment we might be fighting for our lives. We were delirious with excitement. Our Lieutenant Debussy sent out a small reconnoitering force under Lejaune, and it was the good luck of our escouade to be selected for this duty. Within half an hour we were advancing *en tirailleurs* over the loose, hot sand.

"Are we the bait of a trap? Or would you call us the point of a spear?" said Michael, marching between Digby and me.

"Both," replied Digby. "A bit of meat on the end of a spear. . . ."

There was no doubt, however, that Sergeant Major Lejaune knew his job. On a low, rocky hill we halted and rested, all except Lejaune himself and the scouts whom he sent to distant sand hills which, while visible from the detachment, gave a wide range of vision in the supposed direction of the enemy.

Among others set to similar tasks I was ordered to watch one particular man and to report any movement on his part. I watched the tiny distant figure through the shimmering heat haze which danced over the sand until my eyes ached. Upon opening them after one of these rests, suddenly I saw that he was crawling back from his position. Once below the skyline he rose and ran, stooping, then halted and signaled: ENEMY IN SIGHT.

Lejaune was notified, and he sent a man running to an eminence well to our left rear. Soon we were lining the edge of our plateau, concealed and waiting. A few minutes later, the man who had been sent off fired a shot and exposed himself on the top of his hillock. To my surprise, I saw our scouts retiring—not back to us, but to him. Then I saw a flutter of white on a distant hill.

Rallying round the man who was firing from the top of the rock, the scouts opened fire at distant camel-mounted figures who began to appear over the sand hills. We received no orders, save that we should lie as flat as the hot stones that concealed us.

The scattered fringe of Arabs increased to lines, and the lines to masses of swiftly moving riders, and soon their cry of "*Ul-ul-ul-ullah Akbar*" came to our ears like the roar of an advancing sea. As they came, the little party of scouts fired rapidly, and after about the thousand-yard range a camel would occasionally sprawl to the ground, or a white-clad figure fall like a sack on the sand.

Yet on swept the Arabs, the men in front firing from the saddle, the others brandishing their swords and waving their lances aloft. Rapidly and steadily the little band of scouts fired, and by now every bullet was hitting man or beast in the closely packed horde.

Then one by one our scouts fled to the right rear, each man dropping and firing as his neighbor rose to retreat. Before long they were again in position, more in line with, yet still farther behind us. With increased yells, the Arabs swerved to their left and bore down upon them. I could scarcely keep still. None of the scouts had been hit, but in a couple of minutes they would be overwhelmed by the wave and outnumbered fifty to one.

As I held my breath, the tiny handful again rose, turned their backs and fled toward a sand hill in our rear. With a yell of mingled execration and triumph, the Arab harka swerved again and bore down upon their prey.

Then Sergeant Major Lejaune stood up on a rock, gave an order coolly as on parade, and, at less than fifty yards, the Arab masses received the withering blast of our magazine fire. Swiftly as our hands could move the bolts of our rifles, we fired and fired again into the surging mob that halted, retired, then fled, leaving half their number behind.

But these were by no means all dead, or even wounded, and our orgy of slaughter rapidly turned into a hand-to-hand fight. The dismounted Arabs, knowing they must die, had but the one idea of gaining paradise in the slaying of an infidel. With a shout of "*Baïonette au canon!*" Lejaune had us to our feet and launched in a bayonet charge down the slope. The Arab swordsmen were rallying to the attack on foot, but our disciplined rush swept them back.

They broke and fled, and Lejaune soon had a double rank of kneeling and standing men shooting them down. Before long the only Arabs in sight were those that lay in the little bloodstained heaps.

It was a neat action, reflecting the highest credit on Lejaune and on Corporal Dupré, who was in charge of the scouts. The latter was the next day promoted to sergeant, and Sergeant Major Lejaune made adjudant.

Such was my first experience of war, my first blooding. I had killed one man with cold steel and I think at least three with my rifle. Reflecting on this, I was glad to remember that these Tuaregs were human wolves, professional murderers whose livelihood was robbery with violence and torture.

I found afterward that Digby had had his coat torn under the armpit by a spear, which, as he remarked, was not wear, but tear, on a good coat. He had shot his assailant at a half-inch range, and was troubled with doubts as to whether this would be considered sporting in the best Arab circles.

Michael, being a noted winner of bayonet competitions, had used the butt of his rifle in the melee, and seemed to think it unfair of the Arab to wear a turban, which diminishes the effectiveness of this form of fighting. However, neither of them was hurt, nor were any of our friends.

Having buried the dead, we retired toward El Rasa, weary but pleased with ourselves, to make our report.

THE PITCHED BATTLE of El Rasa was fought next day, our battalion holding the oasis against tremendous odds until supports came from the brigade. Then the Arabs learned what quick-firing mule guns can do against a mob of advancing horse and camel men.

As my part in this battle was confined to lying behind a palm tree and shooting whenever I had something to shoot at, I have no adventures to relate. I might as well have spent the day on a rifle range. But after our victory, we proceeded southward, the weeks that followed being a nightmare of marching that ended in the worse nightmare of garrison duty at Zinderneuf. Here we had the initial misfortune of losing Digby and many of our friends, including Hank and Buddy. They departed to the mounted-infantry school at Tanout-Azzal, where Legionnaires were taught the art of handling and riding mules. This separation was a cruel blow to Michael and me, but we felt certain we would be reunited sooner or later. Meanwhile, there was nothing to do but to make the best of this and the other miseries of Zinderneuf.

THINGS BEGAN BADLY in this ill-omened mud fort, isolated in the desert like a tiny island in the midst of an ocean. Cafard, the desert madness, broke out early, and in very virulent forms, both suicidal and homicidal. Captain Renouf, our Commandant, shot himself after a month of life in that dreadful oven. Within a week, a corporal killed a sergeant and then committed suicide. These were most unfortunate affairs, for both the captain and the corporal were on the side of the angels and were decent, fair-minded people.

But the fates had one more disaster in store before they launched upon our luckless heads the final torrent of destruction. Lieutenant Debussy, the new Commandant, sickened and died, and his place was taken by none other than Adjudant Lejaune.

From this moment the atmosphere of Zinderneuf changed from bad to worse and rapidly from worse to the worst possible. The lion tamer had entered the cage, and the lions, sullen, desperate, knew that he held in one hand the whip that would drive them to revolt and in the other the revolver that would punish them at the first sign of it. In fact, life at Zinderneuf became not really life so much as the avoidance of death—death from sunstroke, madness or Adjudant Lejaune.

Michael and I realized that mutiny among the men would soon be inevitable. In that case, we should have the choice of fighting for the hated Lejaune, together with Sergeant Dupré and Corporal Boldini, or of joining a gang of traitors.

SURE ENOUGH, ONE NIGHT the huge, hairy ruffian Schwartz came to me as I sat in a cool corner of our little courtyard. He would have made a great pirate captain, for he was endowed with brains and determination, unhampered by scruples. He had also a power of command. "Are you enjoying life, Smith?" he asked, seating himself beside me. "Would you like a change?"

"I am fond of change."

"Have you ever seen a pig die?"

"No."

"You soon will."

"Feeling ill?" I inquired. I did not like the gross Schwartz.

"You are going to see a big pig die," he went on. "An adjudant pig. *Monsieur le Cochon* is going to become *Monsieur Porc*."

"And are you going to become Mr. Pork Butcher?"

"That remains to be seen," growled the German. "So many want a slice of the pork that we shall have to cast lots."

For a minute he sat silently, gnawing his knuckles. He was shaking from head to foot with fever or excitement. Then, "Do you want a chance to be *charcutier?*" he asked.

"I have had no experience—"

"Look you," he growled, seizing my arm, "you will have the experience shortly, *either as pig or butcher*. All here will be cochon or charcutier in a day or two. Choose and tell your brother to choose. . . . Meantime, if any man comes to you and says 'Porc,' reply 'Cochon.' Then he will know that I have spoken to you, and you will know that he is one of us. We don't care which way you make up your minds. There are enough of us, oh, enough . . ." And, as somebody approached, he got up and slouched off.

That night I told Michael what I had heard.

The next day it was Guantaio. I was sitting in the same place and he crept toward me purposefully.

"It's hot," he said, removing his kepi and puffing, as he sat down beside me. "Are you fond of hot . . . porc?"

"Cochon!" I playfully said.

"Ah! What do you think of it all?"

"I never think."

This silenced him for a minute. Then he said, "They are ten to one. What chance has a big pig and one or two biggish pigs against a score of butchers?"

"Ah!" I said imitatively. "What do you think of it all?"

"I never think either," said Guantaio, with a malevolent smile. Then, nudging me, he said, "How would you and your brother like to be pigs if I could find two or three other pigs to join the big and biggish pigs?"

I belied my statement that I never thought, and did some rapid thinking. Was it his task to find out whether my name was to be put on the butcher list or on the pig list? Were all those who did not wholeheartedly join the butchers to be shot in their beds on the night of the mutiny? Or was the rogue trying to find out which was the stronger party in order to betray his friends if he thought them likely to lose?

"How should we like to become pigs, you say?" I temporized. "I should hate to be butchered, shouldn't you?"

"Very much," he replied. "But I have heard of pigs attacking men. *Taking them unawares* and eating them up."

"I should hate to be eaten by a pig, shouldn't you?"

"Very much," he agreed. "One does not want to be slaughtered by butchers nor eaten by pigs."

"Need either happen?"

"Not if one is a wise pig—forewarned and forearmed."

"And are you going to warn the pigs?"

"I don't know."

I had a conviction that he was speaking the truth, for there was a ring of genuine doubt in his voice. I decided he was simply trying to find out where his interests lay. Would it pay him better to assist his friends or his superiors?

That he was one of the ringleaders of the plot was obvious, since he was the bosom friend of Colonna, Gotto, and the rest of Schwartz's band. But he probably saw the dangers attendant on mutiny. It might fail. Even if it succeeded, it could only lead to a terrible march into the desert. On the other hand, reward and promotion were certain for the man who saved the lives of his superiors and the honor of the flag. It would be simple for Lejaune and a few supporters to defeat the conspirators. They need only enter the barrack room at night, seize the arms and arrest the suspects. Anyone resisting could be shot immediately. Lejaune alone could do the business with his revolver, if all were asleep. I began to wonder why Guantaio should be hesitating. Surely it was to his interest to betray his friends?

Then a light began to dawn upon me. This Guantaio was the henchman of his compatriot Corporal Boldini. Boldini might be killed when the mutineers killed Lejaune, for Boldini was hated second only to Lejaune himself. Suppose the Italians, Guantaio, Colonna and Gotto, were a united party led by Boldini, with some sinister end of their own in view? In other words, suppose they hoped to steal the jewel?

Undoubtedly they believed Boldini's story that Michael carried about a priceless gem to which they had as much right as he. No, I decided, Guantaio spoke the truth when he said he did not know what to do. He was a knave all through. What he really wanted to do was to follow the course most likely to leave him in possession of two things—a whole skin and a share in the jewel—unless indeed he could get the jewel itself.

"It's a difficult problem, my friend," I said. "One does not know which side to take. One would like to be a pig, if the pigs are going to catch the butchers napping. . . . On the other hand, one would like to be a charcutier, if the butchers are going to act first. And that is the point! When *are* the butchers going to kill?"

"*Monsieur le Grand Charcutier*" (by whom, I supposed, he meant Schwartz) "talks of waiting till full moon. A few haven't joined yet, and Schwartz would like to get everybody. If he can't, he wants to know exactly who is to be killed before they start, so there won't be any accidents. The date of the full moon would be good for him. Do it at night and have the moon for long marches, rest in the heat of the day."

"So one has three or four days to make up one's mind?"

"Yes, but I don't advise you to wait. Schwartz will want to know in good time, so as to arrange some butchers for each pig."

"And Lejaune?" I asked. "Suppose somebody warned him?"

"Who *would?* Wouldn't his death be a blessing to all?"

"Not if things went wrong," I replied. "Nor if it ended in our dying in the desert."

"No," agreed Guantaio, gnawing away at his nails. "I hate the desert. . . . I fear it. . . ."

Yes—that was the truth. He feared being involved in a successful mutiny almost as much as an unsuccessful one.

"Suppose, *par exemple*, I warned Lejaune?" I asked.

"Huh! He'd give you sixty days and take care you never came out alive. And he would know what he knows already—that everybody hates him and would be delighted to kill him, given the opportunity. . . . And what would your comrades do to you?" He laughed most unpleasantly.

No, I decided, Guantaio would not like me to warn Lejaune. If Lejaune were to be warned, he preferred to do it himself.

"How would they know that I was the informer?" I asked.

"Because I should tell them. If Lejaune knows, then it will be you who told him."

So that was it? Guantaio could turn informer, having sworn that I was going to do so! Not only would he save his own skin, but Michael would soon have a brother the less when Schwartz heard who had betrayed him.

"Of course, you and your brother would be held to have acted together, as you always do," said Guantaio.

So that was it again? We having been denounced as traitors, Guantaio, secure in his role as executioner of justice, might then murder and rob Michael without fearing the fate of Bolidar.

"What would you do if you were me?" I asked.

"Join the butchers. Better the enmity of Lejaune than half the barrack room led by Schwartz. Lejaune couldn't come straight to your bed and murder you, but Schwartz could. And he *will*, unless you join him."

Obviously this creature spoke from minute to minute as new ideas occurred to him. At present he saw the desirability of me and Michael being mutineers, though before he had seen some advantage in our not being of their party.

"I shall talk it over with my brother," I said, "and we will give you our answer tomorrow. Probably we shall warn Lejaune. Tell Schwartz that. Then he can do as he pleases."

His eyes lit up. Our defying Schwartz seemed to suit him. "You won't warn Lejaune until you have told Schwartz you are going to do so?" he asked.

"No—provided there'll be no mutiny tonight."

"Oh, no. Not until the full moon."

As soon as he went away, I knew that the first thing to do was to talk with Michael. I found him in the barrack room, putting away his rifle and kit after sentry go. Together we went back to sit on the *angareb*, and I told him all that had happened.

"Position's this, I think," he said, when I had finished. "Schwartz and his band propose to murder Lejaune and anybody who stands by him. Guantaio has given the show away to Boldini because he thinks the mutiny too risky, and Boldini wants to join the mutineers if they're successful—but not otherwise. He, Guantaio, Colonna, Gotto and perhaps Bolidar are in league to get the 'diamond' one way or the other. If we join the mutineers, Boldini and company will join, too, hoping to kill and rob me in the desert. If we refuse to join the mutineers, Boldini would then get Guantaio to murder me in my bed—ostensibly for being a traitor to the cause—and pinch the 'great diamond' from my belt. Failing that, Boldini would use us in helping to suppress the mutiny, hoping that in the scrap I might get done in and he could rob my corpse. He could even arrange it."

"On the other hand," said I, "Boldini may know nothing about the plot. Guantaio may be wondering whether to let the mutiny go on, or to warn his old pal Boldini and give the show away."

"Quite," agreed Michael. "We're absolutely in the dark with congenital liars like Guantaio, but, on the whole, the swine seems to be egging you on to join the plot. That means he has some personal interest in our joining it."

"What's to be done, Beau?"

"Get together an opposition gang, then tell Schwartz that we are going to warn Lejaune."

"Exactly," said I. "I am sure Saint-André will stand with us. He is a loyal Frenchman. But suppose we can get no one else?"

"Then we and Saint-André will warn Lejaune and tell him he can count on us three."

"Of course, Schwartz and company will try to do us in as traitors," I observed.

"Probably," agreed Michael. "But if we can get up a strongish party, Schwartz's lot may chuck the whole idea of mutiny. If they don't, it will be a case of who strikes first. We must warn Lejaune the moment we've made it clear to Schwartz that we're going to do so."

We sat silent for a minute. Then, "Tell you what," Michael said, "we'll call a meeting. Tomorrow evening at six, the other side of the oasis. We'll invite Saint-André and any other Frenchmen who might follow him. Then there's Maris, Dobroff, Glock and Ramon among the foreigners who might join us. How I wish Digby, Hank and Buddy were here. As it is, we shall just have to get all those who are not actually of Schwartz's gang."

"I'll bring whom I can," I said. "Six o'clock tomorrow, beyond the oasis."

NEXT EVENING, ABOUT SIXTEEN of the better sort assembled near the shadoof in the shade of the palm grove, out of sight of the fort. There were enough of us, as Michael remarked to me, to control events, provided a united party could be formed. This proved impossible. Michael addressed the meeting first, explaining the situation and the necessity to tell Schwartz that the mad scheme must be abandoned. But here his speech was interrupted.

"*No treachery!*" roared Marigny, a grizzled old soldier, honest but brainless, who admired Schwartz and loathed Lejaune.

"Don't bray like that, my good ass," said Michael. "Where is the treachery in telling Schwartz, 'We are opposed to your murder gang—so drop the idea at once'?"

"I say it *is* betrayal, to tell an accursed dog like Lejaune that they are plotting against him."

Michael sighed. "Well, what are you going to do, Marigny?"

"I'm for Schwartz."

"A slinking murderer? I thought you were a soldier—of sorts."

"I'm for Schwartz," he said again.

"Then go to him. Get out. We should prefer it, being neither cowards nor murderers."

Marigny flushed, put his hand to his bayonet, and made as though to spring at my brother; but he evidently thought better of it as Michael closed his right hand and regarded the point of Marigny's chin. With a snarl of "Dirty traitors!" the old soldier turned and strode away.

"Anybody else think as he does?" asked Michael.

"I can't betray Schwartz," said Blanc, a rotund, black-eyed Marseille seaman. "I can't join Lejaune's bootlickers."

"Then join Schwartz's assassins," said Michael. "You may be safer there."

Blanc departed grumbling.

"I must join my compatriots, I'm afraid," said Glock.

"You are 'afraid'!" mocked Michael. "It is Schwartz you are afraid of. But you'd be safer outside that gang."

"I can't betray my compatriots."

"Well, can you go to them and say, 'I don't believe in murder and I am certain this business will end in the deaths of *all* of us, unless you drop it'? Can you do that?"

Big, simple Glock could only scratch his head and shuffle from one foot to another. "They'd kill me."

"They certainly will kill you—of thirst, if you let them lead you out there," argued Michael, waving to the encompassing desert.

"It seems we've all got to die, either way," said Glock.

"That's what I am trying to prevent. If the decent men of this garrison would tell Schwartz to stop, no one need die."

"Except those whom *Lejaune* is killing every day," said Cordier, a clever and agreeable Frenchman who had been a doctor and whose treatment his comrades preferred to those of any army surgeon. "If that cur could be shot with safety, I'd do it myself and become a benefactor of the human race."

"Where do *you* stand then?" asked Michael.

"With you and Saint-André," replied Cordier, "though I admit my sympathies are with Schwartz. Still, one's been a gentleman."

And in the end we found that only Cordier, Saint-André and our old friend Maris could really be depended upon to join us against Schwartz. One by one the others went off, some apologetic, some blustering, some honestly anxious to support what they considered Schwartz's brave blow for their rights.

When we five were alone, Michael said, "Well, I'm afraid we're not going to scare Schwartz off his scheme."

"No," agreed Cordier. "It looks more as though we're only going to provide him with more little pigs."

"There won't be any pigs if Lejaune acts promptly," said Saint-André.

Maris agreed. "He has the five of us, plus Boldini and Dupré— unless Boldini is in with the mutineers."

"Yes, seven of us," mused Michael, "even without Boldini. That is an ample force. It is simply a matter of acting a night before Schwartz. There need be no bloodshed either."

"Fancy fighting to protect *Lejaune!*" Cordier smiled. "Enough to make *le bon Dieu* giggle. But anyway, who'll tell Schwartz and offer him the chance to drop the whole thing?"

"I will," said Michael.

"We all will," said I. "We'll go to him together. We won't emphasize the fact that we speak for ourselves only."

And so the five of us agreed.

As we strolled toward the fort, we met a man carrying pails for water. It was the Portuguese, Bolidar, who had been so roughly handled in our barrack room at Sidi-bel-Abbès. As he passed Michael and me, he half stopped, winked, made as though to speak, then went on. Looking back, we saw that he had put his pails down and was signaling to us.

Michael asked Saint-André and the others to go on to the barrack room and do nothing until he returned; then we went back toward the oasis, where Bolidar was waiting.

At first Bolidar was incoherent; it was clear that he was in a very unbalanced state. "My friends," he gabbled, "I can bear it no longer. My conscience. My sense of gratitude . . . On that terrible night when I was so cruelly misjudged, you tried to save me. . . ."

"Well, what is it you want to tell us?" asked Michael.

"Your diamond!" whispered Bolidar, gripping Michael's wrist. "Lejaune means to get it. And he'll kill me! If he doesn't Schwartz will . . . or Boldini. . . . What shall I do!"

Realizing that terror was driving him to unburden himself, we never doubted the truth of what he was saying. He oozed truth from every pore, and he showed it in every gleam of his bloodshot rolling eyes, every gesticulation of his trembling yellow hands.

Michael patted the poor rascal's shoulder. "There, there, no one's going to kill you. You join our party and you'll be safe enough."

"*Your* party?" asked Bolidar. "What is *your* party?"

"The stoutest fellows in the garrison. We're going to *warn* Lejaune if Schwartz doesn't agree to give up the murder."

Bolidar threw his hands up and shook with mirthless laughter. "*But Lejaune knows!*" he cried. "*He knows who's in it and when it's to be, and every word that's said.*"

Michael and I stared at each other aghast.

"Who tells him?" asked Michael.

"*I do,*" was the proud reply. "And when he has got your diamond, he will kill me."

I was staggered. If Lejaune knew all about it, what of our threat to Schwartz? What was our position now?

"Why doesn't Lejaune do something?" asked Michael.

"Oh, he'll *do* something all right," said Bolidar. "He'll do a good deal, the night before Schwartz and his fools intend to strike. But he waits to see what you two are going to do. If you join Schwartz, I am to be loyal and enter the barrack room with Lejaune and the others in the night. As we cover the mutineers with our rifles, mine is to go off and kill you. But if you don't join Schwartz, I am to be a mutineer, and when *you* enter the barrack room with Lejaune I am to shoot you from my bed. Either way you are to die—and, after getting the diamond for Lejaune, I am sure to die too. . . . Oh, God!"

"And suppose I remain neutral?" asked Michael.

"Then I am to harangue the mutineers and urge them to kill

you as a nonsupporter! You and any others that don't join. That way it will not look as though I have any personal motive. I am to offer to 'execute' you. Having done it, I am to get the diamond and give it to Lejaune. Yes," he added with another whispered gasp, "and Lejaune is going to shoot me if I don't secure the jewel!" He rocked his body to and fro in despair.

"Is Boldini in this?" Michael asked sharply.

"Well, Boldini told Lejaune about the diamond in the first place. Both hope that you two are going to help them arrest the mutineers. That is, if you refuse to join Schwartz. But Boldini and Lejaune don't trust each other, Guantaio says. He tells me that Boldini now intends to get the diamond for himself, instead of for Lejaune, and that Lejaune suspects as much."

"Let's get this clear," Michael said. "You are Lejaune's man. You have kept Lejaune up-to-date with every development. Lejaune has given you the job of killing me and getting the diamond, no matter whose side I join. Now, how does Boldini intend to get the diamond?"

"Guantaio once told me that he wanted me to join Boldini's gang with himself, Colonna and Gotto. After the mutineers had been arrested and either shot (in self-defense, of course) or put in cells, we were to kill Lejaune *and* those who stood by him. Once we had the diamond we could decide whether to liberate the mutineers and use them in fighting our way to Morocco, or whether their mouths should be closed. We could set fire to the fort, clear out, and everything would be blamed on the Arabs."

"And why did you not fall in with this pretty scheme?"

"Who could trust Boldini? Or Guantaio? Or any of them, for that matter? Once Boldini had the diamond, to be one of the syndicate would be death! Even to know who had got it would be death. How can one work with such dishonest people?"

"Quite," said Michael. "It must be a great handicap."

"It is," agreed Bolidar, and he meandered on about the untrustworthiness of Italians.

"Well, now, let's get down to business," Michael interrupted. "What do you want us to do?"

"I thought that if I told you two all about it—the real truth to honest men—you would save my life and your own, and give me a share in the diamond."

"How save our lives?"

"All desert together before the mutiny. Then you give me a third part in the diamond when we are safe."

"How do you know we should keep our promise?"

"Because you are English. In Portugal, we say, 'Word of an Englishman!' when we are swearing to keep faith."

"That is very touching," said Michael. "But suppose I give you my word that I haven't got a diamond?"

Bolidar smiled greasily, as at one who must have his little jest. "Oh, señor!" he murmured, waggling his head idiotically. "One knows of the little parcel in your belt pouch."

"Oh, one does, does one? Fancy that!"

Silence fell.

"Anyway we might make a party," suggested Bolidar. "It is known that Saint-André, Maris, and one or two others refuse to listen to Schwartz."

"But they are not deserters," said Michael.

"No, but when they know that they are to be killed, what then? Lejaune is going to have no survivors of this mutiny, whichever side they may be on. He's going to have the diamond and the credit of saving the fort single-handed. It will end in wealth and promotion for him, but death for everybody else. Death, I tell you. *Death! Death! Death!*" and Bolidar began slavering like a trapped beast.

"All the same, we're not going to desert," said Michael calmly. "So what's to be done? I wonder if one could persuade Lejaune that there is no such thing as a diamond in Zinderneuf?"

"What? Pretend you hid it at Sidi-bel-Abbès?" said Bolidar.

Michael laughed. "No. I merely say I have not got a diamond here—'word of an Englishman.'"

"It's a chance," whispered Bolidar. "Dear Christ! It's a chance! I'll tell Lejaune you left it at Sidi."

"Tell him what you like."

"I'll try it," Bolidar said, rising. "I'll tell you what he says."

"You'll tell us *something*, I've no doubt," replied Michael, as the heroic Portuguese took up his pails and slunk off.

"Well, my son, a bit involved, what?" said my brother as we were left in solitude.

"True," I said. "So let's consider what happens next. Lejaune won't believe the diamond has been left at Sidi and he will raid the barrack room the night before the mutiny anyway. We shall either be in bed as though mutineers, or we shall be ordered to join the guard of loyal men who are to arrest the mutineers. In either case, Bolidar is to shoot you. So directly he starts to raise his rifle, you must shoot him. At the same time, I shall shoot Lejaune myself. (We shall both have to take our rifles into bed with us if we are left with the mutineers.) Next—"

"Next, the fat will be in the fire," interrupted Michael. "What can we do but bolt into the desert if you kill Lejaune? You'd be the most wanted of all the mutineers. Besides, murdering Lejaune is exactly what Schwartz is going to do, and what we object to."

And it was so, of course. I might just as well go to Schwartz and offer to be the butcher. We pondered the delightful situation.

"What *is* to be done then?" I said at last.

"*Nothing*. We can only wait on events and do what's best as they arise. Meanwhile, let's hold polite converse with the merry Schwartz."

We got up and strolled through the starlit darkness to the fort. "I suppose Sergeant Dupré knows all about the plot?" I said, as we passed into the stifling courtyard.

"No doubt of it. Lejaune will want the loyalty of both Boldini and Dupré until he has dealt with the mutineers."

As we entered the barrack room, we saw that a committee meeting of the butcher party was in session. They stared hostilely at Michael and me. I sat on my bed and got out my cleaning rags preparatory to astiquage, and Michael went over to where the conspirators were grouped at the long table. "Have you come with your answer to that question about cochons?" growled Schwartz.

"I have come with some news about a cochon."

Half a dozen pairs of eyes glared at him, and I strolled over. So did Saint-André from his cot. Just then Maris and Cordier entered, and I beckoned to them.

"Lejaune knows all about it," said Michael.

Schwartz sprang to his feet, his eyes blazing, teeth gleaming. "You have told him! You treacherous filthy cur!"

"And come straight here to tell you?" sneered Michael. "If you were as clever as you are noisy, you might see I should hardly do that."

Schwartz stared in amazement, struck dumb that a person should have the courage to taunt *him*.

Michael turned to the rest of Schwartz's familiars. "A remarkable leader," he said. "Here you are making your plans, and Lejaune knows every word you say, almost as soon as you say it. . . . Join you? No, thanks. You have talked cleverly about pigs, but what about a lot of silly *sheep?*" As they sat openmouthed, he continued, "Well, what are you going to do? Whatever it is, Lejaune will do it first. So you'd better do nothing."

"And Lejaune will do it first," I put in.

Michael had won. They knew he spoke the truth, and they knew he had not betrayed them to Lejaune.

I watched Guantaio, and decided that save for a little courage he was another Bolidar. Probably Boldini and Lejaune would hear of Michael's action as soon as Guantaio could get away from his dupes.

"What to do!" murmured Schwartz. "What to do!"

"Declare the whole thing off," said Michael. "Then the noble soul who has told Lejaune so much can tell him that too," and Michael's eye rested on Guantaio—so long, in fact, that that gentleman felt constrained to leap to his feet and bluster.

"Do you *dare* to suggest—"

"I did not know I had suggested anything," said Michael.

"If it is you," growled Schwartz, glaring at Guantaio, "I'll hang you to the wall with bayonets through your ears."

"He lies! He lies!" screamed Guantaio.

"I haven't said anything," replied Michael. "It is only you who have said it. . . ."

Michael's coolness was establishing a kind of supremacy over these stupid creatures who stared at each other and at us.

"What's to be done?" said Schwartz. "By God," he roared, shaking his fists above his shaggy head, "when I catch the traitor—"

"Take my advice and drop this lunacy," said Michael, "and you may hear nothing more of it."

"Anyhow—Lejaune *knows*, and he's got us," put in Brandt. "I vote we all join the plot, then abandon it. He can't put the whole blasted garrison in his cells."

"Abandon the whole scheme," agreed another. "Then find out the traitor and give him a night he'll remember."

But Schwartz was of a different fiber. "Abandon nothing!" he roared, springing to his feet. "I tell you I—"

"Silence, you noisy fool," said Michael quietly. "Don't you understand *yet* that whatever you say will go straight to Lejaune?"

Schwartz, foaming, swung round on Guantaio. "Get out," he growled, pointing to the door.

"I swear I—" began Guantaio.

"Get out, I say! And when the time comes—be careful. Let me only *suspect* you, and I'll hang you to the flagstaff by one foot."

Guantaio slunk off.

"Now listen to me again," said Michael. "If Lejaune had not known about your plot, I was going to tell him anyway."

Schwartz growled and rose to his feet again.

"However, I was going to warn you first," Michael went on, "to give you a chance to think better of it—in which case I should have said nothing. But get this clear. If I learn of any *new* schemes I shall tell him. Understand?"

"You cursed spy! You—"

"Oh, don't be such a nuisance," interrupted Michael. "My friends and I don't choose to die because of your foolishness. We have as much right to live as you."

"*Live*," snarled Brandt. "D'you call *this* living?"

"We aren't dying of thirst in the desert. And even if we are hounded by Lejaune, it's better than being hounded by a company of goums or Tuaregs."

"And who *are* your precious friends?" asked Schwartz.

"There are five of them here, for a start," said Saint-André.

"And how many more?"

"You'll find that out when you start mutinying, my friend," said Maris. "Don't fancy that all your band mean all they say."

"You cowardly hounds!" growled Schwartz. "There isn't a *man* in the place. . . ."

"Oh, quite," agreed Michael. "But we've enough pluck to stick things out while Lejaune is in command, if *you* haven't. Anyhow, now you know how things stand," and he strolled off. The rest of us followed, leaving the butcher party to continue its discussions as best it could at the long table.

CHAPTER 6: A TIME OF DESPERATION

AFTER COMPLETING our astiquage for the morrow, Michael and I strolled out to the courtyard. Within seconds, someone passed us in the dark, then waited near the lantern by the quarter guard, to identify us by its lights. It was Schwartz.

"See here, you," he said, as we drew level. "What are you going to do if someone kills Lejaune without consulting your lordships?"

"Nothing," replied Michael, as Schwartz followed us away from the light. "We shall continue as soldiers. We shall obey the orders of the senior person remaining true to the flag. If you desert, you desert. But if we can prevent mutiny and murder we shall."

"Oh, you will, will you, Mr. Preacher?" replied Schwartz, evidently putting great restraint upon himself. "What I want to know is whether your cowardly gang is going to fight us?"

"Certainly—if ordered to."

"And if there is no one to order you?"

"Then obviously we shall not be ordered to, my good ass. And we certainly shan't hinder your departure."

Schwartz turned to go. "Look to yourselves, I warn you!" he growled. "Look to yourselves."

As we watched Schwartz disappear, Michael said, "They'll do it tonight. Let's have another word with Bolidar. Then we can fix a place of action."

A search of the fort produced no sign of Bolidar, but we tracked him down in the barrack room. He was deep in conclave with Schwartz and his gang at the long table. Eventually, however, the party broke up and Bolidar was left sitting at a bench, polishing his bayonet. I went over to him and said, "Will you polish mine too?" Then, as I gave it to him, I whispered, "Follow me out."

I strolled back to my cot and, taking my mug, went out as though for water. There in the darkness I watched the lighted doorway and soon Bolidar came out.

"Lejaune does not believe that the diamond is not here," he told me, as we huddled together. "The mutineers are going to shoot him and all the noncoms on morning parade tomorrow. They think he will be expecting it at night, and he'll be off guard. They are going to kill Dupré and Boldini simultaneously. If your party is a big one they are going to leave you alone, if you leave them alone. Blanc, who has been a sailor, is going to lead them to Morocco by Lejaune's compass. They will court-martial Guantaio, the dirty traitor, and if he is found guilty they will hang him."

"And you?" I asked.

"I am to shoot Lejaune—to prove my sincerity. If I don't, I am to be shot myself. Guantaio has been maligning me to Schwartz."

"Have you told Lejaune this?"

"I am just going to do so now," he replied, and I gasped.

"Then he'll arrest them tonight?"

"Probably. If he believes me."

"But what if he doesn't?" At that the wretch had another nerve storm and I had to quiet him down. "Look here," said I. "My brother and I will save you, provided you do nothing against us. We'll prevent the mutiny, and nobody will be killed."

He clutched my hand—and I hoped I spoke the truth.

As Bolidar slunk off, I went back to the barrack room. There, taking my Arabic copy of the Koran from the shelf above my bed, I seated myself beside Michael. I began to read in Arabic, as we often did. But, between verses, I passed on the news in the same language, as though still reading. Just as I was closing the book, Bolidar reentered the room and began to undress.

"What about my bayonet, Bolidar?" I called.

"Oh—half a minute, Smith," and he began polishing it.

When he brought it over, he bent over my bed to hang the weapon on its hook, and whispered, "I cannot find him. Will tell him tomorrow," and went back to his place.

Under cover of the lights-out bugle, I repeated this to Michael.

"Then we shall have a quiet night," said he, and silence descended in the room as usual.

LYING IN MY COT, I realized that I could not share Michael's faith. What more likely than that Lejaune should choose tonight for his counterstroke? He could hardly continue to sit on the powder barrel when the fuse was alight.

I tried to put myself in Lejaune's place. What should I do if I were he, in such circumstances; if I wished first to save my life, and secondly to secure a gem reposing in the pouch of one of the two or three men upon whom I could depend in time of trouble?

For hours I tossed and turned in my hot uncomfortable bed as the problem tossed and turned in my hot uncomfortable brain. In desperation for sleep, I turned again, this time facing the door. And there, in the doorway stood—Lejaune.

He was quite alone and, as he looked from bed to bed, he held a revolver in his hand. Whom was he going to shoot?

Without thinking, I raised myself on my elbow. He saw me at once. Placing a finger to his lips, he beckoned to me. I stared in amazement. Frowning savagely, he beckoned again with an imperious movement of his arm.

Was he going to murder me outside? Was he going to tell me to fetch Michael out? As these thoughts flashed through my mind, I struggled into my trousers and tunic and tiptoed to the door.

"Follow me," said Lejaune, and led the way to his quarters. Closing the door of his bare little room and seating himself at the table, he stared at me with an evil-tempered frown. "Do you and your miserable brother want to live?" he suddenly growled.

"On the whole, I think so, mon Adjudant," I replied.

"On the whole, you do," sneered Lejaune. "Well, you'd better listen carefully, for only I can save you. There's talk of a jewel your gang got away with in London. Also there is a plot among those dogs in there to murder you both and steal it, and desert with it."

"Is that so, mon Adjudant?"

"Don't you answer me! God smite you, you unspeakable corruption! I know all about it, as I know everything else that is done, said, and even thought in this place. I don't care a curse what becomes of you and your brother; but I won't have plots and murders in any force under *my* command. D'you hear me, sacred animal?"

"I hear you, mon Adjudant."

"I am going to teach these curs to attend to their duty and leave diamonds and plots alone. To that end, I am going to detail you and your brother and a few more—say, Legionnaires Saint-André, Cordier and Maris—as a corporal's guard to arrest the ringleaders. You'll act at my orders, and you'll shoot down any man I tell you to shoot—as mutineering mad dogs *should* be shot. And to prevent any more disturbances, your brother will hand over this diamond to me. I'll put it where no plots will trouble it. You and your cursed jewels! Wrecking discipline and causing trouble! You ought to be doing twenty years in jail, the pair of you. D'you hear me?"

"I hear you, mon Adjudant."

"Shortly you and your brother and the others will be given ammunition. You two brothers will be put over the magazine, and will shoot *anyone*, except myself, who approaches it. I'll teach the swine to mutiny—by God, I'll teach them! It was your brother I wanted, but you happened to be awake and I saw no point in entering that cage of treacherous hyenas. So go back and wake your brother, Saint-André, Maris and Cordier, and tell them to get up quietly and come out with their rifles. I shall be at the door with my revolver and I'll shoot anybody who makes a move I don't like. Now, go!"

I saluted and turned about.

So the hour had come! Lejaune was going to make *us* the executioners. And it was our duty to obey him. But Michael? What would happen when Michael denied any knowledge of a diamond?

"Make a sound and you'll be the first to die, the first of many, I hope," growled Lejaune, and I felt his revolver jabbed into the small of my back as I went down the passage.

We reached the door of our barrack room, where the Adjutant halted, his revolver raised. I crept to Michael's bed and whispered in his ear, "Beau, old chap! . . . It's John. . . . Don't make a noise. . . ." He woke, and was instantly alert. "Get dressed, take your rifle and bayonet and go out. Lejaune is relying on our party."

He saw Lejaune in the doorway near the night lamp, and got off his cot. I crept to the others, and by the time I had roused them Michael was creeping from the room, dressed, his rifle in his hand. I saw Lejaune give him some cartridges, then I crept out too, taking my rifle and bayonet.

"Go outside and load," whispered Lejaune, giving me ten cartridges. "Then shoot any man that sets his foot on the floor."

We charged our magazines and stood behind Lejaune in the doorway, rifles ready, while Saint-André, Maris and Cordier joined us. Not one of the sleepers stirred.

"Saint-André and Cordier, remain here until relieved," Lejaune said. "If any man wakes, cover him with your rifle, and say you'll shoot him if he leaves his bed. Do it at once, if he disobeys. Fail, and I'll shoot you myself. Follow me, you others," and he quietly led us back to his quarters.

"Guard the door," he said to Maris, "and shoot anybody who approaches." Then, ushering my brother and me into the room and closing the door, he said, "Give me the wretched diamond that is the cause of all this trouble." He glared at Michael. "Out with it, you scurvy hound, unless you want your throat cut by those mad dogs who've fixed *your* business for this morning at parade. Yes, I know all about it. *Quick*, I say . . ." and he shook his fist.

Michael stared in astonishment. "'Diamond,' Monsieur . . . ?"

Lejaune's eyes blazed. "You try any tricks with me and I'll blow your filthy head off!" He picked up his revolver from the table where he had laid it. "Give me that diamond. D'you think I'm going to have discipline spoiled by every cursed jewel thief that chooses to hide here with his swag?"

"I have no diamond, mon Adjudant," replied Michael quietly.

"As I could have told you, mon Adjudant," I put in, "my brother has never had a diamond in his life."

Words failed Lejaune. I thought (and hoped) that he was going to have an apoplectic fit. His red face went purple and he drew back his lips, baring his teeth and causing his mustache to bristle. He raised and pointed the revolver, and I was about to bring up my rifle, but I knew he could shoot twice before I could even cover him. I was thankful that Michael and I had sufficient restraint to stand motionless at attention.

I told myself that Lejaune needed us alive for the present. At any moment we might hear the rifles of Saint-André and Cordier, as the mutineers rushed them. Or the mutineers might burst into the room to kill him. Yet he was a brave man. Situated as he was, his life hanging by a thread, he still attended to the business in hand. He turned his glare from Michael to me.

"Oh? You would talk, would you?" he said, in a sinister tone. "Well, you haven't much more time for talking. Just a little prayer, perhaps?" and he turned his revolver from Michael's face to mine, and back again to Michael's.

It was most unpleasant, the twitching finger of a homicidal maniac on the hair trigger of a loaded revolver a yard from one's face. He began to swear blasphemously, horribly.

Then, without thought, I did what would have been the bravest thing of my life if it had been done consciously. I defied Lejaune! "Look here, Lejaune," said I coolly. "Don't be a silly fool. In about two minutes you may be hanging on that wall with bayonets through your hands. We've got no diamond and you've got five good men to fight for you, more's the pity! So stop gibbering about jewels and be thankful that we know *our* duty, if you don't."

"*Very* Stout Fella," murmured my brother. "Order of Michael for you, John."

For a moment Lejaune just looked faint. Then, with a howl, he sprang toward me—but as he did so Michael's left hand made a swoop, passed under Lejaune's hand and swept the revolver to the floor. As it clattered to the ground, my bayonet was at

Lejaune's throat and my finger was on the trigger. "Move and I'll kill you," I hissed, feeling like a cinema star and an ass.

Michael picked up the revolver.

"So you *are* mutineers, you loyal lying swine," panted Lejaune, moving his head from side to side, and drawing deep breaths as though choking.

"Not at all," said Michael. "We're soldiers wishing to do our duty, not babble about diamonds. Man, don't you know this fort will be burned, the garrison gone and you dead in an hour's time, unless you do your job while you've a chance? . . ."

"You'll do your duty all right," snarled Lejaune, "and afterward, when I've filled your mouths full of salt and sand, *en crapaudine*, perhaps you'll prefer drops of water to diamonds. Perhaps it will not be I who jabbers about jewels then, eh?"

"Your turn to jabber now, anyhow, Lejaune," said I wearily. "But what about stopping this revolt?"

The man pulled himself together. "Come with me," he said, with a certain dignity. "Our real conversation is postponed until I have dealt with a few other unspeakables. Put that rifle down."

I lowered my rifle and opened the door. Michael put the revolver on the table and Lejaune took it up. Maris, on guard outside, looked at me inquiringly.

"Follow me, you three," Lejaune said.

At the door of the barrack room stood Saint-André and Cordier.

"No one has moved, mon Adjudant," reported Saint-André.

"Put down your rifles," said Lejaune to us three, "and bring all arms out of this room, quickly and silently. You other two will shoot any man who leaves his bed."

We set to work, emptying the arms rack of the Lebel rifles first, then going from bed to bed and removing the bayonets from their hooks. A steel bayonet scabbard struck a tin mug, and a man sat up. It was Vogué.

"Cover him," said Lejaune, and the two rifles turned toward the startled man. Vogué fell back instantly and closed his eyes.

On my last journey to the door, with a double armful of bayonets, one slipped and fell. As it did so, I shot out my foot. The bayonet struck it and made little noise, but my foot knocked against a cot and its occupant sprang up, blinking.

"*Himmel!* What's that?" It was Glock.

"Lie down," I whispered, nodding toward the door.

"Shoot him if he moves," said Lejaune.

Glock lay down again, staring at Lejaune as might a hypnotized rabbit at a snake. In another minute there was not a weapon in the room, nor was there a sound. And none slept so deeply as Corporal Boldini, who was nearest to the door.

Lejaune took a key from his pocket. "To the armory with the rifles, quick! You, Saint-André, mount guard. Send the key back to me with Cordier and Maris, and shoot anyone who approaches the place, other than one of these four.

"Now then," he continued to Michael and me, as the others crept off, laden with rifles, "some of these swine are awake, so keep your eyes open. If several jump at once, shoot Schwartz and Brandt first. If only one moves, leave him to me."

A faint lightening of the darkness outside the windows showed that the false dawn was breaking. As I stared into the room, I found myself wondering what Lejaune would do next. What indeed should I do if he ordered me to open fire on unarmed men in their beds? What would Michael do? Private conscience said, Sheer murder! but military conscience said, Your duty is to obey your officer.

The windows grew lighter. Maris and Cordier crept back, their work completed, and Maris gave Lejaune the key of the armory. "Saint-André is guarding the magazine, mon Adjudant," whispered he, saluting.

"Come with me, Smith," Lejaune said to me, "and I'll disarm the guard and sentries. You other three remain here. Shoot instantly any man who puts his foot to the ground." He glared round the room. "Aha, my little birds, you'd plot against me, l'Adjudant Lejaune, would you? . . . Ah! . . ."

I followed him down the passage.

"I'll clear that sentry off the roof first," he said. "Then there'll be no shooting down on us when I disarm the guard."

Leading the way, he went up the stairs that opened onto the flat roof, round which ran a thick, low wall, embrasured for rifle fire. After relieving the sentry on patrol, he posted me. He then took the man's rifle and ordered him to go below to the guard-room and ask Sergeant Dupré to come up to the roof.

"Now," he said to me as the man went, "come here." He pointed down into the courtyard to the open door of the guard-room. "I shall order Sergeant Dupré to take the rifles of the guard and sentries, then send one man out of the guardhouse with the lot. Shoot anybody who comes through that doorway, if he does not have half a dozen rifles."

Raising my rifle, I covered the doorway. I saw the relieved sentry cross the courtyard and enter the guardroom, and a moment later Sergeant Dupré came out.

"Watch!" growled Lejaune. "That sentry will talk, and they may make a rush."

Nothing stirred.

Sergeant Dupré came up to the roof and saluted.

"I want the rifles of the guard and sentries, Sergeant Dupré," said Lejaune. "Shoot any man who hesitates. Send one man, and only one, to me here, with the lot."

Sergeant Dupré turned about and descended the stairs, crossed the courtyard and took the rifle from the sentry at the gate. The man preceded him to the guardroom; then he visited the other sentries, repeating the procedure.

A minute after the Sergeant's last visit to the guardroom, a man came out. I was relieved to see that he carried three or four rifles over each shoulder, the muzzles in his hands.

"Watch," growled Lejaune. "They may all rush out together now. Open rapid fire if they do," and he also covered the door-way with the rifle he had taken from the sentry.

The man with the rifles, one Gronau, a big stupid Alsatian, came up the stairs. I did not look round, but kept my eyes fixed on the doorway through which a yellow light struggled with that of the dawn. Then I heard a crash behind me. I wheeled, expecting to see that the man had felled Lejaune from behind.

Gronau had released the rifles with a crash, and was pointing, staring, his mouth wide open. So obviously was he stricken that Lejaune, instead of knocking him down, turned to look in the direction of his pointing hand.

The oasis was swarming with Arabs!

Even as we looked, a horde of camel riders swept out to the left, another to the right, to surround the fort. There were hundreds of them already in sight, even by this poor light.

Lejaune showed his mettle instantly.

"Back with those rifles!" he barked at Gronau. "Send Sergeant Dupré, quick!" Then he snapped at me, "Down to the barrack room! Give the alarm. Take this key to Saint-André and issue the rifles. Send me the bugler. Jump, or I'll . . ."

I jumped. Rushing down the stairs, I threw the key to Saint-André, who was standing at the door of the magazine. *"Arabs!"* I yelled. "Out with the rifles and ammunition!"

Dashing on, I came to the barrack room. Michael was pointing his rifle at Boldini's head. Maris was covering Schwartz, and Cordier was waving his rifle over the room in general. Everybody was awake, and there was a kind of whispered babel.

I halted, drew breath, then bawled, *"Aux armes! Les Arbis! Les Arbis!"* To Michael and the other two, I cried, *"Up with you— we're surrounded!"* Then I turned to dash back, conscious of a surge of unclad men clambering from their beds, as their jailers rushed after me. Gleeful howls of *"Aux armes! Les Arbis!"* pursued us as the men snatched at their clothes.

Saint-André staggered toward us beneath a huge bundle of rifles. Dupré and the guard were clattering up the stairs, and, as we raced out onto the roof, Lejaune roared, "Stand to! Rapid fire! Give them hell, you devils!" He ordered Dupré to take command of the roof, then went below.

Soon a trickle of men appeared—men in shirt sleeves, men bareheaded and barefooted, men in nothing but their trousers; yet each had a full cartridge pouch, his rifle and bayonet. Within a few minutes everyone was on the roof, and from every embrasure rifles poured their fire upon the Arabs.

It had been a very near thing. But for Gronau, there would not have been a man alive in the place by now.

Below, the plain was dotted with little heaps of white or blue clothing, looking more like scattered bundles of washing than dead men who, a minute before, had yelled ferociously for the blood of the infidel.

Our bugler blew the cease-fire, and as I straightened myself up I looked round. It was a strange sight. At every embrasure was a caricature of a soldier—in some cases almost naked—at his feet a pile of spent cartridges and, in one or two instances, a pool of blood. As I looked, one of them slowly sank to the ground, his head striking with a thud. He appeared to be dead. It was Blanc, the sailor.

"No time yet for shirkers!" shouted Lejaune, striding toward the man. He dragged him from the ground and jerked him heavily into the embrasure. There he posed the body, chest leaning on the upward-sloping parapet and elbows wedged against the edges of the crenellation. Lejaune placed the rifle on top of the embrasure, a dead hand round the grip and a dead cheek against the butt.

"Continue to look useful, my friend, if you can't *be* useful," he jeered. "Perhaps you'll see that route to Morocco if you stare hard enough." Then he called to Boldini: "Corporal, take every third man below, get them fed and dressed. Double back here if you hear a shot, or the assembly blown. If there's no attack, take half of the rest below, then the remainder. Have all standing to again in thirty minutes. Saint-André, Maris, more ammunition. A hundred rounds per man. Cordier, water. Fill all water flasks and put filled pails above the gate. They may try a bonfire against it. Dupré, no wounded will go below. Bring up the medical panniers. Are all prisoners out of the cells?" He glared round. "Where's the excellent Schwartz? Here, you dog, up on the lookout platform and watch those palm trees till the Arabs get you. You'll have a little while up there for thinking out more plots." He laid his hand on his revolver and scowled menacingly at the big German.

Schwartz sprang up the ladder to the high platform that towered above the fort. It was the post of danger.

"Now use your eyes, all of you!" bawled Lejaune. "Shoot as soon as you see anything to shoot at."

Ten minutes later, Boldini returned with the men he had taken below, all dressed as for morning parade. They took their places and the Corporal hurried round the roof, touching each alternate un-uniformed man on the shoulder and ordering him below. Soon they too were back. Now that they were fed, clothed, and reveling in a fight, gone were all signs of cafard and mutiny.

Michael and I went with the third batch, hoping to be back before anything happened. But not a shot broke the stillness as we hastily swallowed soup and tore at our bread.

"They'll never get in here without cannons," Michael murmured, with bulging cheeks.

"What about a regular siege?" I asked. "Even if we kill a score of them to every one we lose, we should be too few to man the walls eventually."

"Maybe we'll get relief from Tokotu."

"A hundred miles away!" I replied. "And no communication."

Michael grinned. "Chance for the *Medaille militaire*," he said. "Go to Lejaune and say, 'Fear not! Alone I will walk through the encircling foe and bring you relief.'"

"Might be done at night, I think," said I.

"I *don't* think. These men will circle the place hand in hand, like a spiritualist's séance, rather than let anyone slip through. Full moon too."

At that point Boldini hounded us back to the roof, and we resumed our stations. All was ready, and the Arabs could come again as soon as they liked.

Lejaune paced round like a tiger in a cage. "Hi you!" he called up to Schwartz. "See anything?"

"Nothing moving, mon Adjudant," replied Schwartz.

A moment later he shouted something, and his voice was drowned in a sudden outbreak of rifle fire from round the fort. The Arabs had lined the sand hills and, lying flat below the crests, were pouring in a steady fire. This was different from their first mad rush, when they hoped to surprise a sleeping fort. They were now difficult to see, and a man firing from his embrasure was as much exposed as an Arab.

As the morning wore on and the sun gained in power, I was increasingly conscious of the heat and of a severe headache. Opposite to me, about a hundred yards distant, was a man who merely appeared as a small black blob every few minutes. He only showed his head when he fired. He, among others, was potting at my embrasure, and with unpleasant frequency there was a sharp blow on the wall near me and sometimes the high wail of a ricochet. Suddenly the man on my right leaped back, shouted, and fell to the ground, his rifle clattering at my feet. I turned and stooped over him. It was the wretched Guantaio, shot through the middle of his face.

As I bent down, I was sent crashing against the wall.

"By God!" roared Lejaune, who had literally sprung at me. "You turn from your place again and I'll blow your head off!" He picked up the moaning Guantaio and wedged him into the place from where he had fallen. "Stay there," he shouted, "or I'll *pin* you up with bayonets."

Suddenly the Arab fire stopped, and our bugles sounded the cease-fire. "Stand easy!" rang out Lejaune's voice. "Wounded lie down where they are." Some half dozen men sank to the ground in their own blood. I was thankful to see that Michael was not among them.

Sergeant Dupré and Cordier went to each in turn with bandages and stimulants.

"Corporal Boldini," barked Lejaune, "take the men down in three batches for soup. Saint-André, replenish ammunition."

When my turn came to go below, I was more thankful for the comparative darkness and coolness of the casern than for the soup and wine even, for my head was splitting.

"A toast to death," said Cordier, as he raised his mug of wine. "This place will be a grave shortly."

"He's fey," said Michael. "Anyhow, better to die fighting than to be done in by Lejaune afterward. If I go, I'd like to take that Adjutant with me."

"He's a topping soldier," I said.

"Great," agreed Michael. "Yet I believe he's torn both ways when a man's hit. The brute says, 'That's one for you, mutineer,' and the soldier says, 'One more of this garrison gone.'"

"He's a beast," I agreed. "He flung two wounded men back into their embrasures—and enjoyed doing it."

"Partly enjoyment and partly tactics. The Tuaregs have no field glasses, and to them a man in an embrasure is a man."

"What about when there are too few to keep up a volume of fire?"

"He hopes for relief before then," put in Saint-André, who had just joined us. "Dupré told me. The wily beggar's kept two goums outside every night since he knew of the conspiracy. They had orders to go hell-for-leather to Tokotu and say the fort was *attacked* the moment they heard a rifle fired, *inside or out*."

"Of course!" I exclaimed. "It would look bad if he had to send for help to quell a mutiny, but he wouldn't mind a column arriving because a goum had erroneously reported an attack."

"That's right. He saves his face and he saves the fort too," said Cordier. "If a shot had been fired at the mutineers, the goums would have scuttled off, and the relief column would have found a heroic Lejaune guarding a gang of mutineers. As it is, they'll know tomorrow morning at Tokotu that the place is invested, and they'll be here the next day."

"Question is—where shall *we* be by then?"

Cordier smiled. "In hell, dear friends."

"Up with you," shouted Boldini, and we hurried back to our stations.

The wounded were again in their places, one or two lying very still in them, others able to stand. On either side of me stood a dead man, his rifle projecting before him, his elbows keeping him in position.

I could see no sign of life in the desert. Nothing but sand and stones over which danced the blinding heat haze.

Suddenly there was a cry from Schwartz on the lookout platform. "The palms!" he shouted. "They're climbing the palms!" He raised his rifle, but those were his last words. A volley rang out and he fell.

Bullets were now striking the *inner* face of the wall against which I stood. Arab marksmen had climbed to the tops of the palms on the other side of the fort, and were firing down upon the roof. Then from all the sand hills the fire broke out again.

"Rapid fire at the palms," shouted Lejaune. "Bring those birds down from their trees. Brandt, up to the lookout platform, quick."

I glanced round as I charged my magazine afresh. Brandt looked at the platform and then at Lejaune. Lejaune's hand went to his revolver, Brandt climbed the ladder and started firing as quickly as he could work his rifle.

Michael was still on his feet, but, as I turned back, I saw his neighbor spin and crash down, clutching both hands at his streaming throat. Soon afterward I heard a shout from above and saw Brandt stagger backward on the high platform. He struck the railing, toppled over and crashed to the roof.

"Find a good place for that carrion, Sergeant Dupré," shouted Lejaune. "Make him ornamental if he can't be useful." Then, "Up you go, Colonna."

Schwartz, Brandt, Colonna! Doubtless the next would be Delarey or Vogué. Then Gotto, Bolidar. Presumably he hoped to keep Saint-André, Cordier, Maris, Michael and me alive until all the mutineers and diamond stealers were dead.

My head ached with eyestrain and heatstroke. Every explosion of my rifle was like a blow on the head with a hammer. I had almost come to the end of my tether when once again the Arab fire slackened and died.

On the sound of the cease-fire bugle, I straightened up and looked round. Michael was all right, but a good half of the garrison was dead or dying. Among the dead were both Sergeant Dupré and Corporal Boldini. Both had been stuck up to simulate living men. Colonna must be dead too, for Delarey had been sent up to the platform, and was lying flat behind a little pile of bodies.

"Saint-André, take rank as corporal," called Lejaune. "All survivors go below for soup and coffee."

Leaving the embrasures to be manned by the dead, we obeyed. Only Lejaune never left the roof, but had soup, coffee and wine brought up to him.

Poor Cordier had spoken truly as concerned his own fate, for he remained at his post, staring with dead eyes across the desert. Maris was dead too. Only three were left—Saint-André, Michael and myself—upon whom Lejaune could rely if the Arabs now abandoned their siege.

But this the Arabs did not do. Leaving a circle of their best marksmen to pick off any defenders of the fort who showed themselves, the bulk of them retired behind the oasis.

Later Lejaune sent Vogué to join the bodies of his fellow conspirators, Schwartz, Colonna and Delarey, on the lookout. Then, except for a crouching sentry in the middle of each wall, those who returned from below sat with their backs to the wall beside their embrasures. The Arab sharpshooters did no harm, and wasted their ammunition on dead men.

And so the evening came and the moon rose. We had permission to sleep, while two sentries patrolled each wall and were changed every two hours. By Lejaune's orders, Vogué pushed the bodies from the lookout platform off to the roof and they were posed in the embrasures. It seemed to give Lejaune special pleasure to thrust his half-smoked cigarette between Schwartz's teeth, and pull the dead man's kepi rakishly to one side.

"He's a devil!" groaned Vogué as he dragged the body of Colonna past me.

"Up with him!" growled Lejaune. "I'll allot your corpse the place next to his, and stick your pipe between your teeth. You are fond of a pipe, Vogué? Helps you to think out plots, eh? Up with him, you dog!" He then sent Vogué back to the lookout platform to be a moonlight target for the Tuaregs.

I had a talk with Michael when we were both below.

"Looks like a thin time tomorrow," said he. "If they pot a few of us and then rush, they should get in."

"If we can stand them off tomorrow, the relief from Tokotu ought to roll up next morning," I said.

"If either of those goums got away and played the game," agreed Michael. "They may have been pinched though. Anyway the relief will find a thin house here, which reminds me that if I take the knock and you don't, I want you to do something for me."

"You can rely on me, Beau."

"There are some letters in my belt—a *public* letter, a letter for Claudia, one for you and one for Digby. And there's a letter and a tiny packet for Aunt Patricia. If you possibly can, sometime get that letter and packet to Aunt. *Especially the letter.* The packet doesn't much matter—it contains nothing of value—but I'd die more comfortable if I knew Aunt was going to get that letter."

"Oh, shut it, Beau," I said roughly. "Your number's not up yet. Don't talk rot."

"I'm only asking you to do something *if* I'm pipped."

"I'll do it if I'm alive," I replied. "But suppose we're both killed?"

"They're addressed and stamped, and it's usual to forward such things found on dead soldiers. Depends on what happens. If we die and Lejaune survives, I doubt their being dispatched, and if the Arabs get in, there's not much chance of anything surviving. But if we're both killed and the relief gets in before the Arabs do, the officer in charge would do the usual thing. We can only hope for the best. . . ." He added, "Anything I can do for you if it's the other way round, John?"

"Well, love to Dig, and there's a letter for Isobel. You might write to her if ever you get back to civilization and say we babbled of her, and sang, 'Just before the battle, Mother,' and all that."

Michael grinned. "I'll say the right things about you to Isobel, old son. But if otherwise, be sure Aunt gets my letter."

When we returned to the roof, the Arabs had ceased firing completely. Only the sight of a little smoke from their campfires and the occasional scent of wood and burning camel dung betrayed their presence. Yet no one doubted that a chain of watchful sentries ringed us. I was ordered on sentry duty and for two hours patrolled my side of the roof with my eyes on the moonlit desert, where nothing moved and whence no sound came.

When relieved, I had a little chat with Saint-André. "Dawn will be the dangerous time; they'll rush us then," he said. "It will want quick shooting to keep them down if they come all together and on all four sides at once. But if they fail at dawn, they'll just pepper us all day and tire us out until the next dawn. They think they have all the time they want."

"Haven't they?"

"No. Lejaune is certain that one of the goums got away. The Arabs couldn't get them *both*, he says. He had them planted at opposite sides of the fort, and half a mile apart."

"What about the Tuaregs' ammunition?"

"The more they spend the more determined they'll be to get ours, and the more likely to put their money on a swift dawn rush with cold steel."

I lay down and fell asleep, to be awakened by the bugle and Lejaune's shout of "Stand to!"

There was no sign of either dawn or Arabs.

From the center of the roof, Lejaune addressed the diminished garrison of Fort Zinderneuf. "Now, my birds," said he, "you're going to *sing*, and sing like the joyous larks you are. We'll let our Arab friends know that we're not only awake, but also merry and bright. First, 'The Marching Song of the Legion.' All together, you warbling water rats . . . *Now*." And, led by his powerful bellow, we sang at the tops of our voices.

Through the Legion's extensive repertoire he took us, and between songs the bugler blew every call he knew.

"Now *laugh*, you merry, carefree, swine—*laugh!* You, Vogué, up there—roar with laughter, or I'll make you roar with pain."

A wretched laugh, like that of a hyena, came down from the lookout platform. It was so mirthless a cackle, and so ludicrous, that we laughed genuinely.

"Now then, you sniggering soup snatchers, laugh in turn," shouted Lejaune. "From the right—you start, Gotto."

And so round that circle of doomed men among the dead ran the crazy laughter, the doomed howling noisily, the dead smiling secretly out to the silent desert.

The Arabs must have gathered that we were cheerful and defiant—for no dawn attack came. Perhaps they just realized there could be no element of surprise; I do not know. But when the sun rose and they again lined the sand hills and opened their heavy fire upon the fort, every embrasure was occupied by an apparently unkillable man, and every Arab who exposed himself paid the penalty.

But not all those who lined the walls of Zinderneuf were beyond scathe. Now and then there would be a cry, a gurgling grunt, and a man would stagger back and fall, or die where he crouched. And, in every case, Lejaune would prop the body in the embrasure whence it had fallen.

As the morning wore on, Lejaune took a rifle, and, crouching beside the dead men, fired several shots from each embrasure, adding to the illusion that the dead were alive. Later still, he set one man to each wall to do the same thing, to pass continually up and down, firing from behind the dead.

When the Arab fire again ceased toward midday, and our bugle blew the cease-fire, I hardly dared to turn round.

With a sigh of relief, I saw Michael among the few who rose from their embrasures at the order, "Stand easy." But of all those who had sprung with cries of joy at the shout, "*Aux armes!*" yesterday morning, only Lejaune, Saint-André, Michael, Vogué, Gotto, Vaerren, three others and I were still alive. The end seemed inevitable. Ten men cannot hold back a thousand.

"Half the men below for soup," ordered Lejaune. "Back as soon as you can," and Saint-André took each alternate man.

Soon soup was ready, although the cook was dead, and we sat at table as though in a dream, surrounded by the tidy beds of dead men.

"Last lap!" said Michael, as I gave him a cigarette. "Last cigarette! Last bowl of soup! Well, well! It's as good an end as any—if a bit early. Look out for the letter, Johnny," and he patted the front of his sash.

"Oh, come off it," I growled. "The relief is halfway here by now. It's as likely that you do my posting for me, Beau."

"No, Johnny. I feel it in my bones. I'm in for it and thank the Lord you're not." He gave my arm a little squeeze above the elbow. (His little grip and squeeze of my arm had been one of my greatest rewards all my life.)

As we returned to the roof, Michael held out his hand. "Good-by, dear old Johnny," he said. "I wish I hadn't dragged you into this, but you'll come out all right. Give my love to Dig."

I wrung his hand. "Good-by, Beau," I replied. "Or rather, au 'voir. Of course, you didn't 'drag' me into this. I had as much right to assume the blame for the Blue Water as you and Dig. And it's been a great lark. . . ."

He patted my shoulder as we clattered up the stairs.

Lejaune assigned one side of the roof to Michael and the opposite one to me. Vogué and Vaerren were sent to the other two. The others went below. Our orders were to patrol the wall and shoot from behind a dead man whenever we saw an Arab.

Lejaune himself went up to the lookout platform with his field glasses and swept the horizon in the direction of Tokotu. Apparently he saw no sign of help.

Nothing moved on the sand hills on my side of the fort, and, as I watched over the heads of my dead comrades, I wondered how much longer this could last, and where on earth all the horrible flies came from.

When the other half of the men returned from below, two men were posted to each wall, Saint-André and Lejaune remaining in the center to support whichever side of the fort should need it most. The Arabs must have been deceived, for they came no nearer and fired impartially at the corpse-guarded embrasures.

Glancing round, as I darted from one embrasure to another, I saw that both Lejaune and Saint-André were in the firing line now, and that Lejaune had one wall to himself. There were only seven of us left. Michael was among them.

The Arab fire died down.

Lejaune himself picked up the bugle and sounded the cease-fire. Saint-André, Gotto and I were sent below to get food, and we spoke not a single word. Saint-André kept dabbing his face with a rag, where a bullet had torn his cheek and ear. When we returned, Michael and the others went down.

Lejaune paced the roof, humming "*C'est la reine Pomare*," to all appearance cool and unconcerned.

Not an Arab was to be seen. Not a shot was fired. I wondered whether they withdrew for meals or for prayers, or whether they fired so many rounds per man, then awaited their reliefs. Certainly it was a leisurely little war—on their side.

A shot rang out. "*Stand to!*" shouted Lejaune, and he blew the assembly, as though calling up reserves to the already well-manned walls. The firing recommenced and grew hotter, and an ominous change took place in the Arab tactics. While a heavy fire was maintained from the crests of the sand hills, men crawled forward en tirailleurs and scratched shallow holes in the sand. Nearer and nearer they came. They were going to assault again.

I rushed from embrasure to embrasure, pausing only long enough to sight my rifle on an Arab. Lejaune was like a man possessed, loading and firing, rushing from one side to the other to empty his gun. . . .

Why from one side to the other? I found myself asking, as I loaded and fired. Then, glancing round, I saw the reason. There was no one defending the two walls that ran to left and right of mine. Lejaune was defending both walls at once, and only one man was defending the wall behind me. Swiftly I looked across.

It was not Michael. Only Lejaune, Saint-André and I were on our feet.

This was the end. . . . Michael was gone. I should follow him in a minute. Cramming another clip into my hot rifle, I looked across again. The opposite wall was now undefended.

Rushing across the roof, Lejaune shouted, "Both walls, damn you!" and I dashed across and emptied my magazine from the other side, a shot from a different embrasure each time. Then back again I ran and got off a burst of fire along the opposite wall. And so Lejaune and I (*Lejaune and I!*) held Fort Zinderneuf, two against a thousand.

When I was nearly spent, panting like a hunted fox and dripping with sweat, the Arab fire again died, and there was silence—a dreadful silence, after hours of racket. Then I heard Lejaune blowing the cease-fire, and bawling orders to his imaginary soldiers.

"Go below, you, quick!" he shouted to me, pointing to the stairs. "Boil coffee and soup, and bring them back here. They may be at us again in a few minutes. If we keep them off till dark, we're saved. . . ."

I stood staring at where Michael lay on his face in a pool of blood.

"Hurry, you swine!" Lejaune roared.

As I dragged myself down the stairs, I saw him posing a corpse in an embrasure. One body still lay where it had fallen. It was Michael's.

I stumbled to the cookhouse. *Keep them off till dark and we're saved*, did he say? I hadn't the faintest desire to be saved. As I struck a match to light the oil stove beneath the soup kettle, I imagined Lejaune posing Michael's body—perhaps before life was out of it. . . . The thought was unbearable, and I turned to run back upstairs.

And as I ran, another thought struck me. Michael's last request and instructions! I must get those letters and the little packet he had spoken about. I must get Lejaune to leave my brother's body to me. After all, things were different now. Lejaune and I were the only survivors.

As I came out onto the roof, Lejaune was bending over Michael. He had unfastened his tunic, torn the lining out of his kepi, removed his sash, and opened the pouch of the money belt. Lying beside Lejaune were three or four letters and a torn envelope. In his hands were a tiny packet, bound up in string and sealing wax, and an opened letter.

I sprang toward him, seeing red, my whole soul ablaze with indignant rage.

"So he had no diamond, had he?" the ruffian jeered, holding up the packet and the letter.

"You damned thief! You foul pariah dog!" I shouted, and, in a second, his revolver was at my face.

"Stand back, swine," he growled. "Back, I say!"

I stepped back and he lowered the revolver. His smile was horrible.

"I didn't know that *men* crept round robbing the dead after a fight, Lejaune," I said. "I thought that was left to Arab women. You dirty cur, you should be picking over dustbins in the Paris gutters, not defiling an honorable uniform."

Lejaune bared his teeth and laughed. "A fine funeral oration from a jewel thief! Any more sentiments before I blow out what brains you have? I don't want to hurry you unduly out of this pleasant world. . . . Oh no, don't think I want you any longer. The Arabs won't attack again today, and a relief column will arrive at dawn. Then you and the rest of these dogs will be given a hole in the sand, and I shall get a captain's commission, and a trip to Paris to be decorated. In Paris, my chatty friend, I shall also dispose of this trifle," and he held up the packet. "A rich man, thanks to you—and to *this*. . . ." And as he said the last word, he kicked Michael's body.

As I snatched at my sword bayonet and leaped forward, my dazed mind took in an incredible fact. *Michael's eyes were open, and turned to me*. Michael was alive! . . .

I would live too, if possible. My hand, still grasping my bayonet, fell to my side.

"Good!" said Lejaune. "Armed attack on a superior officer—and in the face of the enemy! Excellent! I court-martial you myself. I find you guilty and I sentence you to *death. Thus* . . ." and the revolver traveled slowly from my face to the pit of my stomach. "*There!* . . ."

But as Lejaune spoke, Michael's right hand moved. It seized Lejaune's foot. Caught off balance, Lejaune pulled the trigger in the act of looking down. He stumbled, and at the same time I lunged with all my strength and drove my bayonet toward his chest. Then I too fell, and the bayonet was torn from my hand. When I got up, Lejaune was lying on his back, twitching, with the blade of the bayonet through his heart.

Lejaune was dead, and *I* was the butcher after all!

I STOOPED OVER MICHAEL. His eyes were still open. "Stout Fella," he whispered. "Got the letters?"

I told him that he would deliver them in person, that we were the sole survivors; relief would come soon and we should be promoted and decorated.

"For stabbing Lejaune?" He smiled. "Listen, Johnny, I'm for it, all right. Bled white . . . Listen . . . I never stole the sapphire. Tell Dig I said so, and *do* get the letter to Aunt Patricia. . . . You mustn't wait for the relief. . . . When they see Lejaune's body they'll shoot you. . . . Get away . . . in the dark tonight. . . . If you can't, I killed Lejaune. . . . I helped to, anyhow. . . ."

I do not know what I said.

"Listen . . . Those letters . . . Leave one on me . . . in my hand. . . . Confession . . . No need for you and Dig to carry on with the game now. . . . You must get the confession published or it's all spoiled. . . ."

"You've nothing to confess, Beau, old chap," I said. "Half a minute, I'm going to get some brandy. . . ."

His fingers closed weakly on my sleeve. "Don't be an ass, Johnny," he whispered. "Confession's the whole thing. . . . Leave it where it'll be found or I'll haunt you . . . gnaw your neck and go *Boo* in the dark. . . . No, don't go. . . . Promise . . . God! *I'm going blind*. . . . John, where are you? . . . John! . . . John! . . ."

Within two minutes of saving my life, my brother, noble-hearted Beau, was dead.

I could not weep. I have not the gift of tears. But I looked at the revolver still clutched in Lejaune's right hand. . . . It was only a momentary temptation, for I had something to do for Michael. His last words had laid a charge on me, and I would no more fail him when he was dead than I would have when he was alive.

I turned to the letters. One was addressed to Lady Brandon, others to Claudia and Digby, and one to me. Still another was crushed in Lejaune's left hand. The envelope from which he had torn it lay near; it was addressed to the Commissioner of Police, Scotland Yard. Poor Michael's "confession" of something he had never done! I was tempted to destroy it, but his words were still in my ears: I must "get the confession published."

Well, let it remain where it was. It would get enough publicity found in the hand of a murdered Commandant.

I picked up the packet that Lejaune had dropped and put it with three of the letters into my pocket. I then opened the one addressed to me. It ran as follows:

My dear John,

Take the letters with the packet to Brandon Abbas as soon as you can. The one for Aunt Patricia solves the mystery of the Blue Water. Meanwhile, I beg you to see that my "confession" addressed to the Chief of Police is made public. It is what we all bolted for— averting suspicion from innocent people (including your Isobel, don't forget, Johnny boy!). We took the blame between us, and the first of us to die should shoulder the lot. It is not the dead but the living we have to think about, and though you spoiled my plans by your balmy conduct in bunking from home, you can put them right by doing as I say.

Good-by, dear old Stoutest of Stout Fellas. See you in the Happy Hunting Grounds.

Beau

P.S.—Don't come near me there, though, if you destroy that confession.

I put the letter down and looked at his face. It was peaceful, and etherealized beyond its usual strength and beauty. I closed his eyes and folded his hands upon his chest.

A heavy faintness formed the only sensation of which I was now conscious, and I think I must have fallen into a state of semicoma, for I was suddenly aware that a new day was dawning, and, for a minute, I gazed around at the extraordinary sight that met my eyes—the bloodstained roof, the stiff figures crouching in the embrasures, my bayonet protruding from Lejaune's body, and Michael's calm smiling face, as noble in death as in life.

"I must go, Beau, old chap," I said aloud. I knelt and kissed him for the first time since babyhood.

Only then, not till then, did I remember the Arabs! There was no sign of them whatsoever, alive or dead. Yet I should not be doing much for Michael if I walked straight into either their hands or those of the relieving force from Tokotu. Somehow I must evade the entire population of the desert between Zinderneuf and safety. Rising to my feet, I dragged myself down the stairs. I foraged round, filled my water bottle and three big wine bottles with water. Then I emptied my knapsack and haversack of everything but a pair of boots, and filled them to bursting with bread, coffee, and the bottles of water.

After eating and drinking all I could, I shouldered my burdens and returned to the roof for a last look round. There still was no sign of an Arab, though there might have been any number beyond the oasis. I turned to Beau for the last time.

"Good-by, Beau," I said, and as I spoke I almost jumped, for the brooding silence was broken by several successive shots.

Crouching, I ran back to the side of the roof and looked. On a distant sand hill was a man in uniform on a camel. He was waving his arm and firing his revolver in the air. It was a French officer. The relief had arrived from Tokotu.

I must escape, or be tried, and shot, for the murder of my superior officer in the very presence of the enemy. . . .

Yes—but what about this enemy? Was that fellow riding straight into a trap of which the uncaptured fort with its flying flag was the bait? That might be why there had been no dawn assault. The Arabs might have decided that it would be better to maintain the siege, unseen and unheard, and lure any relieving force, by an appearance of safety, into marching gaily into an oasis covered by hundreds of rifles lining neighboring sand hills. They could massacre the relief column and then turn to the fort again.

As these thoughts flashed through my mind, I decided that I must warn the man riding gaily to his death. Seeing the walls lined with soldiers, the flag floating above them, and no sign of an enemy, he would conclude that we had driven them off.

And a whole column must be close behind him. Comrades of ours who had marched day and night to our relief. I could not let them walk into the trap, deceived by the very ruse that had deceived the Arabs. . . .

I decided I must warn this officer, even though it might mean death instead of escape. What to do? Should I run the flag up and down, wave my arms and dance about on the lookout platform? As likely as not, he would take any such signs as signals of welcome. If I were he, until actually fired upon, I should certainly suppose I was safe.

Exactly! *Until fired upon!* Resting my rifle in an embrasure, I aimed as though my life depended on hitting him. I then raised my foresight half an inch and fired. Rushing to another embrasure, I took another shot, this time aiming to hit the ground in front of him. If he walked into an ambush now, he was no officer of the Nineteenth Army Corps of Africa.

He halted. That was enough.

Rushing across to the far side of the roof, I dropped my rifle over, climbed the parapet, then dropped onto the sand. Snatching up my rifle, I ran as hard as I could to the nearest sand hill. If this were occupied I would die fighting, and the sounds of rifle fire would further warn the relief column.

The sand hill was not occupied, and I crept into a deserted Arab trench. From there I could watch the fort and the oasis, unobserved, while I awaited cover of darkness to escape.

As I lay gazing to my front, I was astonished to see the French officer come round the corner of the fort, alone, proceeding as unconcernedly as if he were riding in the streets of Sidi-bel-Abbès! Round the walls he rode, staring up at the dead defenders. Well! I had done my best. I had risked my own safety to warn him. If the Arabs got him and his men now, it was not my fault.

Then I saw that the relieving force was approaching, slowly, carefully, en tirailleurs, preceded by scouts and guarded by flankers. They were handled by somebody more prudent apparently than the officer, and were by no means disposed to walk into an Arab ambush.

Soon I heard the trumpeter summoning the fort. I could imagine the bewilderment of the officer waiting for those gates to open, while the dead stared at him and nothing stirred.

As I waited for him to send somebody in to open the gates, I came to the conclusion that the Arabs must have departed altogether. I wondered whether this had been due to the fort's apparently undiminished garrison, or to news from their scouts of approaching relief. Anyhow, gone they were.

The officer, his sous-officier, the trumpeter and a fourth man now stood in a little group beneath the wall. I gathered that the fourth man was refusing to climb into the fort. The officer drew his revolver and presented it at the man's face. Finally, the trumpeter, his trumpet dangling as he swung himself up, climbed from the back of his camel to a projecting waterspout and through an embrasure. I expected to see him reappear at the gate and admit the others, but he never did. About a quarter of an hour later, the officer himself climbed up and entered the fort. Again I expected to see the gates opened a minute later—but nothing happened.

The minutes dragged by, the relief column stood still as statues, staring at the fort.

Presently I heard the officer inside the fort bawling to the trumpeter. The men outside began to move toward it in attack formation and another squadron arrived on mules. But just then the gates were thrown open from within, and the officer came out alone. He gave some orders and reentered the fort with his second-in-command. A few minutes later, the latter reappeared and evidently gave orders for camping in the oasis.

Before long there would be vedettes posted on all four sides of the fort in a big circle.

After a good look round, I made a bolt to the sand hill behind me. Then, keeping the fort between the oasis and my line of retreat, I carried out a careful retirement until I was half a mile away and among the big stones that crowned a little hill.

Here, beyond the vedette circle, I would be safe until the moon rose, and I could set out on my fairly hopeless journey.

Fairly hopeless? Absolutely hopeless, unless I could secure a camel. Yet killing a vedette to get his beast was nothing better than cold-blooded murder. A more acceptable notion was to try to steal a camel from the oasis during the night. It would be extremely difficult, but I was in uniform, and with bluff and luck it might be done. The luck of course would lie in the camel guard being unaware that I wasn't a member of the relief force. Anyway, I decided to wait until night to see what happened. Then, in spite of the heat and my unutterable misery, I fell asleep.

When I awoke, it was evening. I had been lucky. The nearest vedette was a thousand yards to my right, and so placed that there was no fear of my being seen.

The sun was setting, the heat was waning, and the fort and oasis presented a scene of normal military activity; or rather inactivity, for there was little movement. Here and there a sentry's bayonet gleamed in the oasis, and a column of smoke rose from the palms as a cooking fire was lighted. But inexplicably, so far as I could see, the fort had not been taken over, nor had the dead been removed.

The evening wore on, and I crept nearer the fort. I would wait until most of the men were asleep before entering the oasis and boldly demanding my camel to take a message back to Tokotu.

Meanwhile, from the crest of a sand hill, I saw that the men were parading outside the oasis, and I wondered what this portended. They marched toward the fort, halted, and faced into line. I concluded that their commandant had given them an "off" day after their march, and was now going to work them all night at clearing up the fort and burying the dead. Anyway, he now rode forth on a mule and started to address them.

Suddenly, the man standing beside him cried out and pointed to the fort. I looked too, and very nearly sprang to my feet at what I saw. Zinderneuf was on fire! It had been set alight in several places. What might *this* mean?

Surely it was not by order. No, even as I watched, I was aware of a furtive movement on the roof of the fort. Carefully keeping the gate tower between himself and the troops, a Legionnaire was doing precisely what I had done. I saw his cap as he crept below the parapet. I saw the rifle fall, and a moment later, as a column of smoke shot up, I saw him crawl through the embrasure and drop to the ground.

Who could he be, this Legionnaire who had set fire to the fort? He certainly had my sympathy. I must see that he did not crawl in the direction of the vedette to my right. I began creeping in a direction that would bring me onto his line of retreat in time to warn him.

A few minutes later he saw me, and hitched his rifle forward. Evidently he did not intend to be taken alive—very naturally, after setting fire to one of *Madame la République's* perfectly good forts. I drew out a handkerchief and from the obscurity of a sand valley waved it. I then laid my rifle down and crawled toward him. I noticed that he was wearing a trumpet, slung behind him.

As I came closer, I was conscious of that strange contraction of the scalp which has given rise to the expression, "His hair stood on end with fright." I, myself, was not frightened and my hair did not stand on end, but I grew cold with wonder as I saw what I took to be the ghost of my brother before me, looking perfectly normal and alive.

It *was* my brother—my brother Digby—Michael's twin.

"Hullo, John," said he, as I stared, openmouthed. "I thought you'd be knocking about somewhere. Let's get off to a healthier spot, shall us?" For all his casual manner, he looked white and drawn. His hands were shaking.

"Wounded?" I asked, seeing the state he was in.

"Er—not physically . . . I have just been giving Michael a Viking's Funeral," he replied, biting his lip.

Poor Digby! He loved Michael as much as I did, and he was further bound to him by those strange ties that unite twins. I put my arm across his shoulders as we lay on the sand between two hillocks.

"Poor John!" he said at length, mastering his grief. "It was you who laid him out, of course. You saw him die."

"He died trying to save my life. But he left a job for us to do. I've got a letter for you. Let's get well out of sight and lie low till we can pinch a camel."

I led us clear of the vedettes and nearer to the oasis, giving Digby my story as we went. Soon we were ensconced behind the crest of a sand hill overlooking the oasis and the burning fort.

"Well," said Digby, in a trembling voice, "they're not going to spoil Michael's funeral. Nor are they going to secure any evidence of your neat job on foul Lejaune. They're going to be attacked by Arabs . . ." and he raised his rifle.

"Don't shoot anybody, Dig," I said. These people were now technically our enemies and might soon be our executioners, but they were still our comrades and innocent of offense.

"Not going to—unless it's myself," he replied. "Come on, play Arabs with me," and he fired his rifle, aiming high.

I followed his example, shooting above the head of the officer as I had done once before that day. Again and again we fired, vedettes to left and right of us joining in and showing their zeal by firing briskly at nothing at all—unless it was at each other. It was a sight worth seeing, the retreat of that company. At an order from the officer, they faced about, doubled to the oasis and went to ground, taking cover so that within a couple of minutes there was nothing to be seen but a dark oasis, to approach which was death.

"Good work!" said Digby. "And they can jolly well keep there until the fort is burned out. We'll go in later on and get camels, as vedettes whose camels have been shot by these attacking Arabs."

He then proceeded to give me an account of all his doings, beginning with how his escouade had been ordered from Tanout-Azzal to Tokotu. Here they had found, of all people, the Spahi officer who had once visited Brandon Abbas, now Major de Beaujolais, assigned to duty with mounted units in the Territoire Militaire of the Sudan. The Major had not recognized Digby, of course. It was this very friend of boyhood's days whom I had been trying to warn against what I thought was an ambush.

At Tokotu, news had been received that Zinderneuf was besieged by Tuaregs, and de Beaujolais had set off at once. The rest I knew until the moment when I had seen Digby, de Beaujolais's trumpeter, climb into the fort.

"Well, of course, I was the only one who actually *wanted* to go into the fort," said Digby, "and you know what I saw as soon as I got the chance, so you can imagine what I felt. Leaving Beau's body, I dashed down below and rushed round to see if you were among the wounded, then realized that there *were* no wounded. That meant that you had cleared out, and it crossed my mind that it was probably your bayonet ornamenting Lejaune's body. Anyway, I went dotty. My one idea was to give Beau the funeral I had once promised, then to follow you up.

"Then I heard someone climbing up the wall. I rushed into the punishment cell and hid behind the door. Soon I heard de Beaujolais bawling for me. Later, he and the Sergeant Major actually looked into the cell, but they never saw me. At last, when I felt certain that there was no one about, I crept up to the roof again and took a look. There was a sentry at the gate, and the company was evidently going to camp in the oasis before entering the fort.

"I crawled over to where Beau lay, heaved him up in my arms and carried him below to a bed in the barrack room. All round the cot I laid piles of wood from the cookhouse and drenched it with lamp oil. I did my best to make it a real Viking's Funeral. My chief regret was that I had no Union Jack to drape over him. . . . However, I did the best I could, and covered the pyre with sheets of canvas and a spare Tricolor. It wasn't what I would have liked, but he had fought and died under it, so it served. . . . It served. . . ." Digby's head was nodding as he talked; he was like a somnambulist, and I tried to stop him.

"Shut up, John, I must get it clear. . . . *Oh, Beau! I did my best for you, old chap. . . . There was no shield, nor spear. . . . I had to use your rifle and bayonet to lay beside you. . . . But I did put a dog at your feet!*"

"A dog?" I said. I feared he must be going mad.

"Yes, a dog. A dog crouching with his head beneath his heels. . . . I did not carry it down, as I carried Beau. I took it by one foot and dragged it down. . . ."

"*Lejaune?*"

"Yes. Lejaune—with your bayonet through his heart. Well, when all was ready, what do you think I did, John? . . . *I fell asleep* . . . and slept till evening. . . . I was more my own man when

I woke up. I went to the roof to see what was doing. The company was parading, and I thanked God that I had awakened in time, for in a few minutes they would be marching in to take over.

"I crept back and set fire to Beau's pyre. Then I poured a can of oil over a pile of benches I had heaped up in the next room, and set light to that. I knocked another can over at the foot of the stairs, lit it, bolted up to the stair of the lookout platform, did the same, and by that time it would have taken more water than there is in the whole Sahara to put the place out. I decided it was time for me to shove off." He yawned prodigiously. "So I came to look for you, John . . . to look for . . ."

Digby was asleep. I watched for an hour or two. It was extraordinarily silent. In the oasis even the camels and mules were behaving as though aware that the night was unusual. Not a grunt or bray broke the stillness.

Having decided that Digby had slept long enough, I woke him and said, "What about it? Are we going to have a shot at a camel, or are we going to march?"

"Oh, quite," replied Digby, and went to sleep again in the act of speaking.

This was not helpful, and I was trying to decide whether to give him another hour when I saw two camel riders leave the oasis. I rubbed my eyes. No, there was no doubt about it. Two well-fed, well-watered camels were coming toward us.

I did not for one moment think of shooting their riders, but as the camels drew nearer I crawled down the reverse slope of my sand hill and ran along the valley at its base until I was onto their line. I did not know what I was going to do.

Then suddenly a well-known voice remarked conversationally, "We sure gotta put them wise, Buddy. We don' want nawthen to eventooate to the pore boobs. . . ."

"Hank!" I yelped in glee and thankfulness, and he and Buddy turned their camels toward me.

"Here's *one* of the mystery boys, anyhow," said Hank.

Between two sand hills, Hank and Buddy brought their camels to their knees and dismounted. Both wrung my hand in a painful and most delightful manner. "Excusin' a personal question," said Buddy, "but was it you as had the accident with the cigar lighter an' caused arsonical proceedin's?"

"No," I said. "It was Digby."

"Then I would shore like to shake him by the hand," said Hank. "Is he around?"

"Having a nap over there," I replied.

"The other bright boy, too?" asked Buddy. "An' where's Lejaune? Hev you taken Poppa by the ear an' led him out into the garden to admire the fire?"

As quickly as possible, I told him what had happened—of Michael's death and "funeral."

"He was all wool an' a yard wide," said Buddy, and I felt Michael might have had worse epitaphs.

A brief silence fell upon us. Then, "Gee!" said Hank. "Such nice quiet boys too. Always behavin' like they was at a party. Then one of 'em kills the Big Noise an' the other sets the whole gosh-dinged outfit afire."

As I led the admiring Americans to where Digby was sleeping, I asked where they were going.

"Wal, we was sent lookin' fer some fellas from Tokotu," replied Hank. "Ole Man Bojolly allows they'll run into an Injun ambush if they ain't put wise. I wonder the Injuns didn't git you two when they shot us up," he added.

"We were the Arabs," I confessed with modest pride. "We shot rapid fire, then the vedettes obligingly joined in."

"Gee!" admired Buddy. "And that lyin' Schneider swore he shot seven of you himself. Thinks he oughta get a medal! . . ."

I had difficulty rousing poor Digby, but when he realized that Hank and Buddy were present in the flesh, he was soon very much awake.

"Say, boys," he went on, after greeting them and hearing their tale, "do you think you could be attacked by about a hundred and fifty of us Arabs, and lose your camels? . . . They'd be shot beneath you. You would have peace with honor, and we'd have a chance to save our lives."

Hank looked at Buddy, then said, "Fergit it, son."

I was surprised and disappointed, more at the attitude than at the loss of the camels.

"We won't *fight* you for them," said Digby, "but I wish it had been someone else."

"Why someone else?" asked Hank. "Don't you like us?"

"Yes, but just at the moment I like your camels better."

"Well, then—you got the lot, ain't you?" said Hank.

"Do you mean *you're coming with us?*" I asked, astonished.

"You shore said a mouthful, bo," replied Hank. "Did you figger we'd leave you innercent children to wander about this sinful world on your lone?"

"After you killed the Big Noise and obliterized their block-house?" put in Buddy. "'Twouldn't be right. Well, we figger you're two bright boys but you ain't got no chance on a lone trail. You don't know alkali sagebrush from frijoles. You couldn't tell mesquite from a pinto hoss. Therefore we gotta come along."

"Shore thing," agreed Hank, "and time we vamoosed too, or we'll hev these Senegaleses a-treadin' on us."

A minute later each of the camels bore two riders, and we were padding off at a steady eight miles an hour.

"Any pertickler direction?" said Hank, behind whom I was riding. "London? N'York? Morocker? All the same ter me."

"What about it, Dig?" said I. "We've got to get out of French territory. . . ."

"And where's water?" replied Digby. "I should say the nearest oasis would be a sound objective."

"If there's a pursuit, they'd take the line northwest for Morocco," I pointed out. "I vote for the opposite direction and a beady eye on our fellowman. Where there are Arabs there'll be water somewhere about."

"Shore," said Hank. "But first turn Injun, see? Git Injun glad rags, and live like they does. We're well armed and got our health an' strength an' hoss sense."

From which I gathered that Hank firmly advocated our early metamorphosis into Arabs and the adoption of Arab methods of subsistence. We should not only turn Arab, but should prey upon the Tuareg as the Tuareg preyed upon the ordinary desert dweller. It seemed a sound plan, if difficult of application. However, I had infinite faith in the resourcefulness and courage of the two Americans, and reflected that if anybody could escape from this predicament it was these men, familiar with the almost equally terrible American deserts.

"I vote we go southwest," said Digby. "We're bound to strike British territory and fetch up in Nigeria sooner or later."

CHAPTER 8: AN END TO WANDERING

I COULD FILL a volume with the account of our adventures on this ride that began at Zinderneuf and ended (for some of us) at Kano in Nigeria.

We rode southwest when we could, and northeast when we must, as when, north of Air, we were captured by Tuaregs on their way to the borders of Morocco. However, the upshot of this particular incident was all for the best. In making our escape, we not only secured ourselves four splendid mehari camels but also four splendid Tuareg costumes. We soon got used to the baggy trousers and even to the blue veils that only Tuaregs wear. In fact, we went native altogether, retaining only our rifles and Digby's trumpet. Even in the rifles we were not guilty of anomaly, for along with heavy Crusader swords and lances of a type unchanged since the days of Abraham, the Tuaregs carried rifles of the latest pattern. Anyway, having become a desperate band of ruffians, we found ourselves far less open to attack by every passing Arab band. And we were less likely to be recognized if pursued from Zinderneuf.

During one terrible year of our travels we made an almost complete circle, being once within two hundred miles of Timbuktu, and later within the same distance of Lake Chad. Sometimes thirst and hunger drove us to join salt or slave caravans (even though they were generally going in the opposite direction to ours). Sometimes we were hunted by gangs larger than our own;

sometimes we were met at villages with rifle fire (being taken, naturally, for what we pretended to be); sometimes we reached an oasis only to find it occupied by French Senegalese—far more dangerous to us than nomadic robbers.

We went to places where Europeans had never been before. And, of course, we could never have survived but for the desert skill of Hank and Buddy, though the ready wits of Digby and our knowledge of Arabic often saved the situation when we were in contact with our fellowman.

At last we found ourselves paralleling a caravan route toward Nigeria. But it was then that, after a month of travel in good heart and high hopes, when we were only four hundred miles from safety, we fell into the hands of the treacherous Tegama, Sultan of Agadès. Although we bluffed our way to freedom, by telling him that we were mischief-makers from the north bent upon raising the desert tribes against the French, our rifles were confiscated. It was their loss which precipitated our ultimate destruction.

A COUPLE OF DAYS after escaping the Sultan's clutches we were riding in a long line abreast, and scouting for signs of human beings or water. Both our waterskins and food bags were nearly empty. Hank was on the right of the line, I next to him and half a mile away, having Buddy on my left, with Digby at the far end, cut off from view behind some rocks.

Looking to my right, I saw Hank, topping a little undulation, suddenly wheel toward me, urging his camel to top speed. As I looked, a crowd of riders swarmed over the skyline. Two or three of them, halting their camels, opened fire.

"Dismount and form squar'," yelled Hank, and we three brought our camels to their knees, made a pretense of getting out rifles from under the saddles, leveled our sticks as though they were guns across the backs of the animals, and awaited death.

"This is whar' we gits what's comin' to us," said Buddy.

The band, Hoggar or Tibbu robbers by the look of them, bore down with yells of "Ul-ul-ul-ullah Akbar!"

I could have wept that we had no rifles. Steady magazine fire would have brought the yelling fiends crashing to earth and provided us with much that we sorely needed. The feeling of utter impotence was horrible. Could Digby escape, or would they see his tracks and follow him after slaughtering us? Would they swerve from our apparently leveled rifles? No. On they came.

And then from somewhere rang out a *bugle call*—that portentous bugle call that had been the last sound so many tribesmen had heard, the call that announced the closing of the trap and the hail of bullets against which no Arab charge could prevail. As the bugle died away, Hank roared orders in French at the top of his voice, and away to the left a man was apparently signaling back to the French forces behind him. The effect was magical. The band swerved to their right, wheeled, and fled—fled to avoid what they thought a terrible trap! Evidently they imagined that the danger was somewhere behind Hank, for they fled past the rocks behind which Digby had blown his bugle.

Suddenly my heart leaped into my throat as one of the robbers swerved to the left and, either in a spirit of vengeance or a native desire for single combat, rode at the man who had exposed himself to signal the French force. "Quick!" I shouted. "He'll get him," and I found myself yelling Digby's name.

We scrambled onto our camels, Hank bawling commands in French, and Buddy yelling devilish war whoops.

Digby stooped, then poised himself like a javelin thrower. As the Arab raised his sword, Digby's arm shot forward and the Arab received the stone full in his face. As the man reeled, Digby sprang at his leg and pulled him down, the two falling together.

They rose simultaneously, the Arab's sword went up, Digby's fist shot out, and we heard the smack as the man fell backward, his sword dropping from his hand. Digby seized it and stood over the robber, who was clawing at the sand.

Then we heard another sound. A rifle was fired, and Digby swayed and fell. An Arab had wheeled from the tail of the fleeing band, fired a shot at thirty yards' range, and fled again.

Digby was dead before I got to him, shot through the back of the head with an expanding bullet.

WE TIED THE FALLEN ARAB'S FEET and then we buried Digby.

"He shore gave his life for ourn," said Hank, chewing his lips as he stood over the grave.

Buddy said nothing, but Buddy wept.

I will say little about my feelings. *Digby was dead. Michael was dead.* I felt that the essential *me* was dead too. I felt like an automaton, a creature sentenced to death, waiting for the blow to fall.

When we moved on, we took the Arab with us, and left him at the first water hole to which we came. From there we rode on with filled waterskins. But Digby's death proved to be the first of a series of disasters that now overtook us.

First we encountered a sandstorm that nearly killed us and obliterated all tracks. We missed the caravan route to Kano. Next, nearly dead with thirst, we reached a water hole, and found it dried up. Here our starving camels ate some poisonous shrub, sickened, and within thirty-six hours were dead.

We thus found ourselves lost in the desert, without rifles, food, camels, and with one goatskin containing about a pint of water. This we decided not to drink until we must literally drink or die.

For a day we struggled on, incredibly, without water, and at the end wondered whether we were not a day's march farther from the caravan road on which were water holes and villages.

Night found us unable to speak, our lips black and cracked, our tongues swollen horribly, and our throats closed. Our mouths were like hard leather, yet on we reeled. Toward morning, I could go no farther and sank down. I tried to rise and failed. Seeing that I could do no more, the other two lay beside me, and we fell asleep.

The sun woke me to see Buddy, with a face like death, staring at a scrap of paper torn from a pocketbook. He passed it to me. On it was scrawled: *Pards. Drink the water slow and push on quick. Buddy, we bin good pards. Hank.*

Hank was gone. . . .

Buddy untied the goatskin, filled his mouth with water, then swallowed slowly. "Take a mouthful like that, then swaller," he croaked. "We don' wanta make what he done all for nix, and he won't come back an' drink it."

I filled my mouth and swallowed—but I could not swallow the lump in my throat.

We staggered on, moistening our mouths at intervals, and just before sunset on the second day saw a mirage of palms, a village, a mosque, and—the mirage was real.

We stayed at this village for months, scouring the desert for Hank, working as water carriers, camel men, and at any other job that was offered, and we were never both asleep at the same time. When French patrols visited the place, we hid, with the sympathy of the villagers.

We could have joined more than one southbound caravan, but I would not urge Buddy to leave. He had absolute faith in the indestructibility of Hank. At first it was: "He'll come mushin' in here termorrer, a-throwin' his feet like the Big Buck Hobo, an' grinnin' fit ter bust. . . ." Then it was: "Nobody couldn't kill Hank. . . . He's what you call ondestructible. . . ." And at last, "Well, you can't stop here fer keeps," he said. "I reckon I bin selfish, but I couldn't leave old Hank while there was a chance."

Had it not been for Michael's letter and my longing to see Isobel, I would have continued to urge Buddy to stay, for that was what he really wanted to do. But we joined a caravan headed south toward Zinder, headquarters of the Territoire Militaire, and left it just before it reached its destination, in case some noncom there might recognize us.

Our adventures between Zinder and the British border were numerous, and our hardships great; but now that I had lost Digby, and Buddy had lost Hank, and neither of us cared much what happened, things went fairly well. And one day we rode, on miserable donkeys, into the city of Kano, and I revealed myself to an astounded Englishman as a compatriot.

He was kindness itself, and put me in communication with a friend of Aunt Patricia's, a Mr. Lawrence of the Nigerian Civil Service. This gentleman sent me money and an invitation to stay with him at his headquarters and to bring Buddy with me.

But when I told Buddy that on the morrow he was going to ride in a train once more—I found that he was not. Having seen me safe to Kano, he was going back to look for Hank! Nothing would shake his determination, and it was a waste of words to try. Nor was it pleasant to strive to persuade him that his friend was dead.

"Would *you* go if it was yore brother that was lost?" he said.

All I could do was to see him fitted out with two fine camels, food, water, ammunition, a small tent, and a Hausa guide recommended by the Kano Englishman. The latter accepted my word that I would repay him for these kindnesses as soon as I saw Mr. Lawrence. I hated parting with the brave, staunch little Buddy, and I wondered if I should ever have had the courage to go back into that hell on such a ghost of a chance of finding a friend. . . .

At Kano I took the train to some place of which I have forgotten the name, and Lawrence met me on the platform. I vaguely remembered him as a quiet, rather dour man whom I had seen two or three times at Brandon Abbas.

He came nearer to showing excitement while he listened to my story than I thought was his wont. When I had finished he said, "And you *still* do not know the rights of this Blue Water mystery?"

"No. I only know that my brother Michael never stole it."

"Quite so," he replied. "And now I have something to tell *you*. Your Major de Beaujolais has told me the whole story of Zinderneuf from *his* side, and about finding your brother's 'confession.' I went on to Brandon Abbas and told Lady Brandon—but it really did not seem to interest her enormously!"

It was incredible to sit there in a hammock chair under the African stars outside this man's tent, a whisky and soda in my hand and a cheroot in my mouth, and hear him tell how *he* had taken our Zinderneuf story to *Brandon Abbas!* But what struck me more was his account of how Aunt Patricia had received his news. Apparently she did not even *want* to get the wretched jewel back.

Lawrence gave me much Brandon Abbas news. Sir Hector Brandon had died miserably of cholera in Kashmir. Claudia had married one of the richest men in England, nearly old enough to be her grandfather. Augustus, always a poor horseman, had fallen off his hunter and been dragged until dead. Isobel was quite well.

No, she had not married. (I was conscious that my heart now functioned more regularly than it had done since the mention of Claudia's marriage.) Mr. Lawrence had heard from Lady Brandon only a month or so ago. She wrote more frequently nowadays. . . .

Isobel was well and unmarried! Did she feel toward me as she had that morning when I did not say good-by to her—that morning so long ago?

And Aunt Patricia knew! Yet what did she know after all? Merely that Michael professed to be the thief of the Blue Water, and that he, and he alone, was to blame. But did she yet know the *truth?*

I HAD BEEN FEELING horribly ill for some time, with a combination of malarial fever and dysentery—that ill-omened union after whose attack a man is never quite the same again. Now I collapsed altogether.

Had I been Lawrence's own son, he could not have done more for me, and though it was a long, slow recovery, the day came at last when I found myself weak and emaciated on Maiduguri platform en route for home.

George Lawrence was with me, having sworn to deliver me safe and sound at Brandon Abbas. I put aside the unworthy thought that it was himself he yearned to see safe and sound at that house— but I could not help noticing that whatever I said interested him only to the extent that it bore upon Aunt Patricia.

And so, one day, I found myself on the deck of a steamer, breathing glorious sea air, and looking back upon the receding coast of Africa. My eyes watered as I realized that I was leaving behind me all that was mortal of two of the finest men that ever lived—my brothers, Michael and Digby. Also two of the finest men of a different kind, Hank and Buddy, who, since no word had come from Kano, were probably dead also. But for Isobel, I should have wished that I were dead too.

Instead, I was glad to be alive, and in my selfishness I let my joy lay balm upon my grief—for in my pocket were cables from Isobel, cables dispatched as soon as Lawrence's letter reached Brandon Abbas, announcing my appearance in Nigeria.

I WILL NOT WRITE OF MY MEETING with her. Those who have loved can imagine something of what I felt as I walked to the Bower— which she had elected to be our meeting place, rather than a railway platform—and found my darling, more beautiful than ever, and if possible, more sweet and loving. Joy does not kill, or I should not have survived that hour.

At first Aunt Patricia was only coldly kind. I was made to feel that she had not forgiven me for the day I had left her house against her express desires. After lunch, as we were sitting in the drawing room, the room from which the Blue Water had disappeared, I gave her the letter and packet.

She opened the letter first, read it, then read aloud in a clear, steady voice:

"My most dear and admired Aunt Patricia,

"When you get this, I shall be dead, and when you have read it I shall be forgiven, I hope, for I did what I thought was best, and what would, in a small measure, repay you for some of your great goodness to me and my brothers.

"My dear Aunt, I knew you had *sold* the Blue Water to the Maharajah (for the benefit of the tenants and the estate), and I knew you must *dread* the return of Sir Hector, and his discovery of the fact, sooner or later.

"I was *inside one of the suits of armor* when you handed the Blue Water over to the vizier or agent of the Maharajah. I heard everything, and when once you had said what you said and I had heard it—it was pointless for me to confess that I knew—but when I found that you had *had a duplicate made*, I thought what a splendid thing it would be if only we *had a burglary* and the Blue Water substitute were stolen! The thieves would be nicely down in the eye, and your sale of the stone *would never be discovered by Sir Hector*.

"Had I known how to get into the Priest's Hole and open the safe, I would have burgled it for you.

"Then Sir Hector's letter came, announcing his return, and I knew that things were desperate and the matter *urgent*. So I spirited away that clever piece of glass, or quartz or whatever it is, and I herewith return it (with apologies). I *nearly* put it back after all, the same night, but I'm glad I didn't. (Tell John this.)

"Now I do beg and pray you to *let Sir Hector go on thinking I am a common thief and stole the Blue Water*—or all this bother that everybody has had will be all for nothing, and I shall have failed to shield you from trouble and annoyance.

"If it is not impertinent, may I say that I think you were absolutely right to sell it, and that the value is a jolly sight better applied to the health and happiness of the tenants and villagers and to the productiveness of the farms, than locked up in a safe, in the form of a shining stone that is of no earthly benefit to anyone.

"It nearly made me regret what I had done when those asses, Digby and John, had the cheek to bolt too. Honestly, it never occurred to me that they would do anything so silly. But I suppose it is selfish of me to want all the blame and all the fun and pleasure of doing a little job for you.

"I do so hope that all has gone well and turned out as I planned. *I bet Uncle Hector was sick!*

"Well, my dear Aunt, I can only pray that I have helped you a little. With sincerest gratitude for all you have done for us,

"Your loving and admiring nephew,

"Beau Geste

"A *beau geste*, indeed," said Aunt Patricia, and for the only time in my life I saw her put her handkerchief to her eyes.

EXTRACT FROM A LETTER from George Lawrence, Esq., C.M.G., of His Majesty's Nigerian Civil Service, to Henri de Beaujolais, Colonel of Spahis, XIXth (African) Army Corps:

. . . And so that is the other side of the story, my friend. Alas, for those two splendid boys, Michael and Digby Geste. . . .

And the remaining piece of news is that I do most sincerely hope that you will be able to come over to England in June.

You are the best man I know, Jolly, and I want you to be my Best Man, a desire heartily shared by Lady Brandon. Fancy, old cabbage, after more than thirty years of devotion! I feel like a boy!

And that fine boy, John, is going to marry the oh so beautiful child whom you remembered. Lady Brandon is being a fairy godmother to them, indeed. I think she feels she is somehow doing something for Michael by smoothing their path so. . . .

Percival Christopher Wren
(1885–1941)

P. C. (PERCIVAL CHRISTOPHER) WREN was born in 1885 in a manor house in Devonshire, England. He was a descendant of Christopher Wren, the architect who designed Saint Paul's Cathedral in London in the seventeenth century. After an education at Oxford University, Wren left England to pursue an adventurous life "on all five continents." He worked his way around the world as a sailor, tramp, schoolmaster, journalist, farm laborer, explorer, and hunter, even working as a vegetable seller in the slums of London. He spent ten years in India, serving as assistant director of education and physical culture in Bombay.

Wren also had a military career. He served for a time in the British cavalry and in the French Foreign Legion in northern Africa. In World War I, Wren joined the Indian army and fought in East Africa, rising to the rank of major before ill health forced his retirement to England. Wren's taste for adventure persisted: He volunteered for a post with the Secret Service in Morocco in 1926, but was rejected.

Wren's first book, *Dew and Mildew*, a novel about India, was published in 1912. From that year until his death, Wren wrote an average of a book a year. In 1924 he published *Beau Geste*. A sensational tale drawing on his experiences in the French Foreign Legion, *Beau Geste* was an enormous success. A dramatization of the book was also popular, and the novel has been made into several movies. Wren wrote many more novels about the Foreign Legion and the Geste family, including *Beau Sabreur*, *Beau Ideal*, and *Good Gestes*.

A tall man with blue eyes, a monocle, and a moustache, Wren was described as "more the retired army officer than the author in appearance and temperament." He had two lifelong hobbies: fencing (he was champion of western India) and tobacco pipes, which he collected from his days as a student at Oxford. When he finally ended his wanderings in the 1920s, Wren settled in his native England.

Critics have characterized Wren's writings as mere adventure stories, but many have praised his lively style and ability to transport the reader into exciting, dangerous places. A biographer wrote of Wren's stories: "There was the breath of life in them, because they reflected the author's eagerness for experience and his ability to report what he had seen."

In 1940 Wren published *Two Feet from Heaven*, a well-received psychological novel. Had he lived longer, he may have moved away from escapist literature into the realm of serious fiction. His travels and adventures had taken their toll on his health, however. After a long illness, Wren died in England on November 23, 1941. He was fifty-six years old.

Other Titles by Percival Christopher Wren

Beau Ideal. New York: Lightyear, 1976.

Beau Sabreur. New York: Lightyear, 1976.

The Desert Heritage. New York: Lightyear, 1976.

The Disappearance of General Jason. New York: Ultramarine, 1972.

Stepsons of France. New York: Ayer.